DEADLY DEALS AND DONUTS

A DONUT TRUCK COZY MYSTERY

CINDY BELL

ISBN-13: 978-1548910495
ISBN-10: 154891049X

CONTENTS

CHAPTER 1

*S*unlight shimmered across the smooth shiny surfaces of the tall buildings and peeked its way down the long city streets. On Green Street, the sound of creaking hinges filled the air, and the aroma of delicious food had already begun to overcome the fumes of the city traffic. Like modern mammoths, trucks of different colors lined the street from beginning to end. In their bellies, delicious breakfast foods cooked and summoned the hunger of everyone within a two-mile radius. Businessmen and women on their way to work in the surrounding buildings would soon arrive in droves to pick up their favorite breakfast burritos, coffees, and donuts. But for the moment, only the vendors bustled up and down the street, opening their trucks and preparing the first meals of the day.

Brenda smiled to herself as she dipped the freshly fried donuts into the sugar and cinnamon mixture. It was a classic donut that was still popular amongst the breakfast crowd. She put the completed donuts aside and grabbed the bowl of dough. She carefully filled a donut pan with the dough, then slid the pan into the oven. The sound of the metal pan as it slid inside gave her a sense of excitement. No matter how often she baked, it always felt like an experiment to her. One ingredient change could create a completely different taste sensation. No matter how many compliments she received on her baking, she was always nervous about whether the customer would like it. It was still new to her to be baking as a profession.

"Good morning, Brenda. I don't know how you beat me here every morning!" Joyce laughed as she climbed the steps into the truck. Her petite frame didn't take up much space, but her boisterous attitude always made her presence known.

"I've already been here for a couple of hours. I just love to get started first thing. There's something about baking in the morning that invigorates me."

"I do like to get up early in the morning, but I

am a bit of a slow starter. I enjoy drinking some coffee and waiting until my toes warm up."

"Until your toes warm up?" Brenda looked over at her with a broad smile.

"Yes, I can't stand to sleep in socks, and my feet always end up sticking out from under the blanket. So, when I wake up in the morning, I have cold feet. After I have my shower, I pour my coffee, and I don't move from the couch until my toes feel warm. Strange, but it's my habit." Joyce laughed as she shrugged her shoulders. "I guess I have built a few of those unbreakable rituals over the years."

"I don't think it's strange, I think it's sweet." Brenda smoothed her shoulder-length brown hair back from her face and wrapped a hair tie around it to create a ponytail. No matter how many times she put it up, it was always slipping free. "I can't stand to sleep in socks either. My husband does, and to be honest, I find it a little creepy. When his feet touch me in the middle of the night, it always wakes me up."

"Ah, the little things we tolerate for love," Joyce said teasingly.

"Yes, if that's all I have to complain about, then I think we're doing pretty good." The oven dinged and Brenda bent over to pull the donuts out of it.

"Oh my, those smell delicious." Joyce took a deep breath of the heavily scented air. "How did the oven warm this morning?"

"It's doing fine so far. I think whatever problems it had have worked themselves out." Brenda gave the door of the oven a light pat. "It's going to do just fine."

"Great. I got such a good deal on it, but I was a little worried. Hopefully, we'll soon be making enough that we can afford to have two ovens in case there's ever a problem with one." Joyce took another deep breath, then laughed. "I'm still so nervous about all of this."

"So far, so good." Brenda set the donuts on the counter to cool. "I'm a little nervous, too, but mostly I'm just so excited to be here, to be honest. I never expected this. It's still sinking in for me. I know it's been a month, but I'm still wrapping my head around it. If it wasn't for you, I never would have had this opportunity." She looked into Joyce's eyes. "Thank you so much."

"No need to thank me, it was your baking skills that drew my attention. When I tasted one of your donuts, I knew without a doubt that you would make the perfect partner in my adventure. I don't say this much about many things, but I do believe it was fate." Joyce's eyes shone as she leaned down to smell the delicious aroma that wafted off the donuts.

"I do, too." Brenda smiled as she shooed her away from the donuts. "They're not ready yet. They need to be glazed."

"It's so hard to resist!" Joyce grinned. To distract herself, she turned to the serving window of the truck.

Cinnamon, coffee, and a variety of tantalizing smells continued to waft up and down the street as all of the early morning trucks prepared their food for the first onslaught of customers. It was still sinking in for Joyce, too, that she'd decided to take such a leap of faith, and she did not regret it for one second. As she opened the register, she was distracted by a strange sound outside the truck. At first she didn't think it was anything, just a subtle knocking, but then it got louder. It sounded like a fist being slammed into metal.

"What is that?" Joyce poked her head out through the serving window and saw a man beside the hot dog truck. He slammed his fist against the door over and over. Because he wore a hooded sweatshirt, she couldn't tell much about him other than his muscular body type.

"We need to talk, Adam!" The roar of one of the

nearby truck engines turning on distorted his voice. When Adam didn't come to the door right away, he started pounding. Finally, Adam opened it and stepped off the truck. He glanced around for a moment, then shoved his hands in his pockets.

"I told you we'd meet later."

"It can't wait until later. I need to know how many pounds."

"Sh!" Adam glanced around and caught sight of Joyce looking out of her truck. "Not here, there are too many people listening. Come inside." He gestured to the truck. As the man turned towards the truck, Joyce got a better view of his features, and she recognized him as Vince Marritelli. Vince stepped inside, then Adam followed after him with another look over his shoulder. Joyce frowned as she ducked her head back inside and looked over at Brenda.

"It looks like Adam's up to something."

"Like what?" Brenda arranged the donuts on a display case.

"I don't know." Joyce sighed and looked back out through the window. Her voice grew heavy as she continued. "I hope it's not what I think it is."

"What would that be?" Brenda wiped her hands and turned to look at Joyce.

"Maybe something to do with drugs?" Joyce winced at the thought.

"That's a big conclusion to jump to. Why would you think that?"

"He's got Vince Marritelli in there with him, and apparently there was once a problem with drugs in the area. It was one of the reasons I hesitated to set up shop here. When I did my due diligence, I found out they conducted a sting here almost two years ago. Some of the trucks were using the food as a cover for selling drugs. Since the police cleared all of that up, I thought it wouldn't be an issue anymore." Joyce frowned and folded her arms across her stomach. "Maybe I should have looked into it more."

"Maybe it's not a problem. We don't know for sure that it is," Brenda reasoned. "I hope that it isn't."

"You're right, I may be overreacting. Vince is a seedy character, but he might have nothing to do with drug dealing. They might have been talking about something else. But we should be extra cautious just in case. I don't want either of us to be at risk. Let's keep our eyes and ears open, all right?" Joyce asked.

"You've got it." Brenda smiled and shrugged.

"With Charlie's job, I've gotten used to doing that. He doesn't like to admit how much danger he's in at times when investigating his stories, but it can be nerve-wracking."

"It must be fun to be married to a journalist. I bet you get some of the inside story before anyone else hears about it." Joyce grinned, relieved to change the subject. "You'll have to keep me up-to-date."

"In some ways it is fun, his schedule is quite flexible, and he is passionate about his work, but in other ways it's not. When he gets caught up in a story, it's hard to get his attention on anything else. But I understand it, he loves his work."

"My Davey was like that when he worked as a police officer. I never expected him home at any specific time, because he always put his all into a case and if a shift needed covering, he'd be the one to take it. He believed he was helping people by wearing that badge."

"And you? What did you think, was he helping people?" Brenda asked.

"I believed that he believed it, and that was all that mattered to me. But it wasn't easy to think of him putting himself at risk, especially when our kids were young. I'm sure you worry about Charlie, too."

"I do. Most of the time he works on financial stories, but often that involves corruption, and that's where things can get a little dangerous. Sometimes he has to upset the wrong people in order to be a great journalist, but that puts him at risk of negative consequences, too. We've talked about it a few times, and he's agreed to be cautious about the stories he investigates. Still, like you said, he's passionate about it and feels like he's making a difference. I don't want to put a stop to that."

"Ah, men and their passions. Lucky for us, our passions are a bit sweeter and far less violent, hmm?" Joyce laughed.

"Ouch!" Brenda exclaimed as she nursed a burn from the side of a pan. "Sometimes less violent."

Soon they were swept up in the rush of customers. By the time they closed up for the day, the register was full and they were both exhausted.

"That was a busy one." Joyce stifled a yawn.

"Yes, it was. Is there anything I can do to help?" Brenda folded up her apron and tucked it into a drawer.

"I'll do the bank drop. If you can take the garbage to the dumpster for me that would be great, but remember, be careful."

"I will be, and you be careful, too."

"No worries, I've got protection." Joyce patted her purse.

Brenda laughed and shook her head. "A can of air freshener is not protection."

"Anything that hits the eyes at the right moment will do just fine." Joyce nodded, then stepped out of the truck. She kept her purse tight against her body as she hurried to her car in the parking lot across the street. Brenda watched from the truck until she knew that Joyce was safe in her car, then she began to gather the trash for the dumpster. It amounted to a small bag. She made sure everything was turned off in the truck, and that all supplies were put away, then she locked up for the night.

When Brenda walked towards the dumpster, she noticed that Adam's truck was still lit up. Sometimes he stayed open late to catch the people who worked longer shifts. She stopped beside the truck to say hello, but when she looked inside, it was empty. However, the metal lids on the hot dog bins were still open. She guessed he might have gone somewhere to dump the liquid from the bins. With a shrug, she headed for the dumpster. Once she tossed the bag inside, she turned around and almost bumped into a man in a hooded sweatshirt.

"Oh, excuse me." She took a swift step back as her heart lurched with fear.

"Watch it!" His eyes were dark and sharp as they focused in on her. "Brenda, right?"

"Yes." She swallowed hard when she recognized him. Vince often hung out with Adam and Pete, the owner of the hamburger truck. She was not surprised that Joyce thought he might be involved in criminal activities like dealing drugs as he was an intimidating character, with a long scar on his cheek and a permanent sneer on his lips.

"What are you doing out here all alone? You should know better. It's dark." He frowned, then glanced over his shoulder.

"It's perfectly safe, usually." She gripped the strap of her purse and watched him closely.

"Not tonight though, is it?" He chuckled. "You didn't expect company, I can tell."

"I'm just closing up the truck for the night, Joyce already took the money to the bank."

"Did you think I was going to rob you?" He shook his head and laughed harder. "Careful how quick you judge, Brenda, you might not know as much as you think."

"I'm just going home." She forced herself to move past him and away from the dumpster. With every step she took, she wondered if he would grab her. When she reached the parking lot, she looked back over her shoulder and saw Vince with Adam beside the dumpster. They seemed deep in conversation. Maybe Vince was right, maybe she did judge too fast, but it was hard not to with how he presented himself. She shuddered at the thought of being alone with him, then climbed into her car.

On the drive home, Brenda received a text from Joyce confirming that the deposit had been made, but that she'd forgotten her tablet in the truck and was going back to pick it up. Once she was parked in her driveway, Brenda texted Joyce back to warn her about Vince hanging out late with Adam. As she stepped out of the car, she tried to leave her worries behind. She opened the front door, and her cheerful six-year-old daughter bounded forward to hug her.

"Oh Sophie, I'm so happy to see you." Brenda hugged her tight.

"Did you bring me donut holes, Mommy?" Sophie grinned.

"Of course."

"What about me?" Charlie stepped into the living room from the kitchen, with a dishtowel in one hand and a bottle of her favorite water in the other. The moment she saw him, she felt as if she was exactly where she wanted to be.

"Yes, I'm happy to see you, too."

"No, I meant did you bring me any donuts? Did you?" He wrapped his arms around her and playfully frisked her in search of the donuts.

"Yes, I did." She laughed as he tickled her, then kissed him. All worries about Vince were erased from her mind as she was embraced by her loving family.

~

*J*oyce made her way back to the truck. Annoyed with herself for forgetting her tablet, she focused on getting in and out while she still had some of her evening left. Most of the time, she had a pretty strict routine. There wasn't anything special about it, but she did enjoy keeping to it. As she passed by the dumpster, she heard voices. To avoid being noticed, she hurried to the truck and stepped inside. However, when she glanced out the window and spotted Adam engaged in an animated conversation with Vince, her curiosity overtook her. She wanted to know what exactly they were talking about.

Through the window, she could see them both as they stood directly under a streetlight. She couldn't hear their voices, but she didn't need to. Growing up with three older brothers, they often plotted against her. As the much smaller and younger sibling, she rarely had a way to defend herself. In order to protect herself, she taught herself to lip read. This allowed her to find out their plans and prank them before they even had the chance to act. It took them a long time to figure out how she always knew exactly what they were up to. As she grew older, she got better and better at it. When she was in college, she took some classes after school to hone her skills and found she was the best in the class. She had found her skills useful throughout the years. Now that she was in her sixties, she still relied on the skill to give her the upper hand when she needed it.

As Joyce stood at the window she could clearly see Adam's lips, but it was harder to see Vince's. It seemed to her that they were discussing merchandise and prices. Her jaw clenched. Had her suspicions been confirmed? Vince was one of the people caught in the net of dealers a couple of years before, however he'd managed to dodge all of the charges. She didn't trust him one bit, and the fact that he was discussing merchandise with Adam concerned her. Adam was a young guy, in his twenties, and seemed to be a decent person, but if he was going to bring drugs on to Green Street again, then she was going to have to do something about it. As the two men parted ways, she grabbed her tablet but waited a few minutes before she stepped out of the truck. She didn't want to risk running into Adam or Vince on the way to her car. Once she thought they were gone, she locked up the truck and walked to the lot.

The entire drive home, her mind was weighed down with what to do about Adam and Vince. Since she was one of the oldest truck owners on the street, she felt a certain sense of protectiveness over the rest of the owners. Although her truck was the new one on the block, everyone seemed to respond to her well. She considered having a meeting to discuss street safety and the need to keep criminal elements away from their location. If the area was deemed dangerous, they would get less and less customers and would be forced to move to another location. As it was, she was certain that Green Street was the best place for her truck. When she stepped into her house, a fluffy ball of fur bounced up to her. She grinned and scooped her up.

"Hey Molly, what are you up to?"

The bunny flicked her ears and stared into Joyce's eyes with that curious gleam that won her over the moment she saw her. "Mmhm, you've gotten into the hay, haven't you? Let's take a look." Joyce stepped into the kitchen to find hay scattered across the floor. "Oh, you naughty bunny, I'm going to have to get you a sitter." She laughed and grabbed the broom to sweep it up. Not long after her husband died, Joyce was introduced to Molly at a local rescue. She'd gone there to pick out a cat or a small dog to keep her company, but the moment she saw the long-eared rabbit, she'd fallen in love.

After Joyce was done cleaning up, she and Molly watched their favorite television show, then she headed to bed. The moment her head hit the pillow, she thought about Adam and Vince and just how she was going to handle the problem. She gazed at the framed photograph of her husband on the nightstand beside the bed. Though it wasn't something she confessed to many people, she still talked to him in the evenings when she couldn't sleep. This night was no different, and soon after she finished telling him about her day, she fell asleep.

CHAPTER 2

When Brenda arrived at the food truck the next morning, she was too preoccupied with her phone to even get the oven started. The weather report was not looking favorable. Although they still did get some customers when it rained, it could potentially knock out two thirds of their revenue for the day.

"Hi Brenda." Joyce climbed the steps into the truck. "How are you today?"

"A little concerned about this rain that we're supposed to have."

"Don't worry, it's going to miss us."

"Are you sure?" Brenda asked hopefully.

"Yes, see?" Joyce held out her tablet for Brenda to see. "The radar shows it going around us."

"Oh good. I was hoping we wouldn't be rained out. You know that councilman is supposed to be meeting with the truck operators today, and I was afraid he would cancel it. Do you know him well?"

Joyce tucked the tablet away into the messenger bag that she wore. "Geoff Pierce? Somewhat. I've seen him a few times, but we've never been properly introduced. He grew up here, but he is younger than my children, so I don't think they ever crossed paths."

"Do you think he's coming here to cause problems or solve them?" Brenda bit into her bottom lip as conspiracy theories swirled through her mind. Charlie was always on a rant about different scandals that involved politicians.

"Honestly?" Joyce laughed. "I think he's coming here for a photo shoot. So he can claim he has his ear to local businesses. But that doesn't bother me, it's free advertising for all of the trucks, and there's nothing better than that."

"Good point."

"Speaking of advertising, I spoke with the artist, Ella, about creating a wrap for the side of the truck. She said it would take about a month."

"For now, our sign will have to do. Did she say anything about a price?"

"Let me check my email, she said she would send through a quote this morning." Joyce pulled out the tablet again. "It's here." She shook her head. "That's a little high." She turned the tablet towards Brenda to show her the email.

"It is. What do you think?"

"Unfortunately, it's the going rate." Joyce shrugged.

"If you think it's too much, we can try to get other quotes."

"No, it's fine. We do want the truck to look professional, and it's a one-time investment. I'm just a bit of a penny-pincher."

"Which is why we're doing so well. I have to say when you first asked me to join you in this, I thought I was crazy for saying yes, but it has really worked out."

"Yes, it has. We're one of the more popular trucks thanks to your baking skills."

"And we're one of the most profitable, thanks to your business sense," Brenda said. "I'd better get to work on the donuts, we're going to have a rush before the councilman's visit."

"He's bringing that events coordinator, Melvin Cooper. Make a special one for them, will you?"

"Special how?"

"I don't know, just something that will make them feel important, maybe pipe a pretty decoration or their names on them, or make them a variety." Joyce smiled. "It doesn't hurt to butter the hands that pull the strings."

"Is that so they won't be able to pull our string?" Brenda grinned through the open side window of the food truck.

"It's always good to plan ahead. Pierce oversees the permits for the food trucks and Melvin is the one with the power to decide whether we get to go to most of the events around town, and it's about time we got bumped higher on that list."

"We are one of the newer trucks, so I guess that explains why we're not chosen too often."

"I know, but that enchilada truck just started a few weeks ago, and it's already been out to the stadium."

"More demand for enchiladas at sports events?" Brenda laughed.

"I suppose, though I'd think they would want something that would cause less fumes in such close quarters."

"Joyce!"

"I'm serious, it could be a distraction for the players."

"You're so funny." Brenda laughed. "Anyway, I'm sure we'll get our turn one of these days."

"Don't be so sure about that, Pierce is buddy buddy with a lot of these owners, and I've noticed that they're the ones that get picked to go to these events. I've seen him, I'm sure he plays favorites and influences Melvin's decisions."

"Well then, we'll just have to become one of his favorites." Brenda winked as she whipped a spoon through the mixture in the bowl she held. "Some extra special donuts coming up."

While Brenda baked, Joyce reviewed the finances of the truck. Everything turned on a hairpin when it came to profit and loss. Luckily, she had enough money to support the truck should it hit some troublesome times, but she would rather see black than red. In the first year after her husband's death, she found it difficult to do anything. Even when she went out, she made it a point to remain alone. The donut truck was her attempt at rejoining the world and giving herself something to focus on. Since Brenda agreed to join her as her baker, she found more than purpose, she found a very good friend. Now that they spent so much time together, she couldn't imagine her life without her. Not long after the donuts were pulled out of the deep fryer, there was a commotion at the front of the line of trucks.

"There they are, see?" Joyce leaned forward so that she could see past the crowd that gathered near the entrance of the street. "That black car is Pierce's. It's so shiny every time I see it. I think he must wash and wax it right before he goes anywhere."

"It is pretty shiny." Brenda peered down the street as well. "But I don't care about that. As long as he does what he promises and protects our right to be here, then he can drive a shiny helicopter for all I care."

"I'm sure he has one of those, too."

"I don't know. Councilmen don't make that much. Do they?"

"They do if they're on the take."

"On the take?" Brenda quirked a brow. "What do you mean by that?"

"Never mind that now, let's get down there and say hello before we lose our chance at convincing them to make us one of their favorites."

"Okay, I'll bring the donuts." Brenda grabbed the box and stepped down out of the truck. As they joined the crowd near the entrance of the street, Brenda could spot the councilman easily. He wore a finely tailored dark suit, and his thick black hair was smoothed down with gel. He was a handsome man, without question, but in a clean-cut way that rarely was attractive to her. He smiled at the crowd before him.

"Hi everyone, so glad to see you again. Most of you know my colleague and friend Melvin Cooper. He's an events coordinator who organizes many of the big events in the area. He asked me to introduce him to some of the concession providers as there are so many new trucks since he was last out here. So, as you know, we're here to sample a bit of everything that everyone has to offer." Pierce patted his stomach. "It's a tough job."

"The donuts, Brenda, the donuts." Joyce nudged her with her elbow.

"Okay." Brenda took a deep breath. She had a hard time putting herself out there in front of other people.

"Go on, Brenda, before Gus gets all of the attention." Joyce looked over at Gus, who stood at the front of the crowd with a platter of fried pickles. Brenda nodded and nudged her way forward through the crowd. When she reached the front, she noticed the man beside Pierce. He was tall like Pierce, but he had a robust stomach and a wicked smirk.

"I can't wait to taste all that you have to offer. If I like it, I'm sure there will be events in your future. And don't worry, even if I'm not too keen on it, I'm sure we can find some events for you, too."

"Mr. Pierce." Brenda cleared her throat. "Joyce and I made a variety of donuts for you and Mr. Cooper to try." She held out the box and hoped that her hands didn't shake. As shy as she was, especially in the face of men with influence like Pierce and Cooper, she predicted that she would find a way to make a mistake.

"Oh, did you? How thoughtful." Pierce smiled as he stepped forward to take the box. "I'm sure they will be delicious."

Brenda lifted the lid of the box as she took a step forward. When she did, her foot collided with something, and she lost her balance. The box went flying out of her hands as she stumbled, then smashed into Pierce's chest when she fell forward into his arms.

"Oh no, I'm so sorry." She straightened up and peeled the box off his chest.

His face was etched in anger for a second as he looked down at two of the heavily glazed donuts that still stuck to his suit jacket. "Well, I'm sure they would have been delicious." He composed himself.

"I must have tripped on something." Brenda

looked back at the pavement behind her, but she didn't see anything she could have tripped over. When she looked up, she caught Gus looking back at her, still clutching his tray of fried pickles.

"I have plenty of napkins here, sir, if you want to try to clean up." Gus gestured towards the napkins.

"Here, I'll help you." Brenda grabbed a few of the napkins.

"No thanks, it's fine, I'll just take it off." He pulled off his jacket.

"We'll get it cleaned for you," Brenda offered.

"Thank you, you can return it to my office once it's cleaned." He handed it to Brenda. "Now, let's try some of those fried pickles, Gus, as if I don't already know how fabulous they are." He chuckled as he walked away from Brenda. She was mortified as she headed back to Joyce's side.

"I'm so sorry, Joyce."

"Don't be, it's not your fault." She crossed her arms as she glared at Gus. "Someone tripped you."

"Are you sure? Did you see it happen?" Brenda looked over her shoulder at Gus as he distributed his pickles. "He wouldn't do that, would he?"

"He would, and he did. We have to look out for ourselves, Brenda, the competition here is fierce. Anyway, give me that jacket." Joyce took it from her. "You make some fresh donuts, I'll keep an eye out for sabotage."

"I really can't believe he did that. I thought Gus was such a nice guy."

"He is a nice guy, in some ways, but when it comes to competition, he's going to do whatever it takes. That's how it is here. You and I, we're doing this mainly for fun. Gus and many of the others here are doing this to survive and support their families."

"But he tripped me. That's such a mean thing to do." Brenda shook her head. "It's like being back in grade school."

"Maybe so, but we can't let it get to us. Don't worry about Pierce. If he didn't like you, he would have done a lot worse. I think he's fond of you actually." Joyce smiled.

"Fond of me? Why?"

"Well, you're very lovable."

"Aw, that's so sweet of you to say, Joyce." She laughed and rolled her eyes. "I guess you're trying to make me feel better."

"It's true." Joyce winked and then looked back at Pierce and Cooper as they made their way along the trucks. "Hurry up with the donuts or we won't get a chance for Cooper to sample them. We could use some of the ones you made before, but they are much more delicious when they are warm."

"Okay, I'm on it, I'm on it." Still nervous from the incident with Pierce, she started to collect ingredients. As soon as she began to stir them together, she relaxed. The soothing motion of mixing the dough and the scent of the spices she added were enough to calm her. By the time the donuts were in the oven, her nerves were settled. She peeked out through the serving window at Joyce, who still stood like a sentry watching the other trucks.

"Hey guys, he's coming this way next." Adam waved to them from the truck beside them. "I know Melvin quite well, I will put in a good word for you. I'll also make sure he's ready for something sweet."

"Thanks Adam." Joyce waved back to him. Adam's truck sold hot dogs of all varieties, along with French fries and soda. He was almost always picked to go to events, which wasn't surprising because his product was popular. Joyce also suspected from the rumors going around amongst the food truck owners that he might have some kind of understanding with Cooper.

"I bet he'll put extra sauerkraut on." Brenda rested her elbows on the counter in the serving window and smiled out at Joyce.

"Yes, he might just do that. Here they come."

Pierce and Cooper stopped at Adam's truck. They exchanged a few pleasantries, then Adam served them some hot dogs. As they ate, Brenda glazed the donuts. She wasn't sure that they would be as good as the first ones she made, as these had been made in a rush and she was upset from tripping earlier, but she hoped the men would like them. She piped 'Donuts on the Move,' the name of the donut truck, on them to make them look fancier and help the name stick in Cooper and Pierce's minds.

Since their truck specialized in an old favorite that was readily available, they tried to put a unique twist on them. Not only did they provide traditional and other varieties of fried donuts, they sold baked donuts as well. It was difficult to compete with the more established businesses for big events like sports games. However, Brenda's healthier baked donuts did help them get into events like office gatherings and children's birthday parties. After the two men ate their hot dogs and sucked down sodas, they made their way to the donut truck. Joyce greeted them with a handshake and a smile.

"Sorry about the incident earlier. We do have some fresh donuts for you to try."

"Nothing to worry about, Joyce, things happen.

I'd love to try some of those donuts." Pierce rubbed his stomach. "But I'm so stuffed from everything else, I'm not sure that I'll be able to eat a bite."

Joyce kept her smile tight on her lips and nodded. "Oh, I understand there are so many delicious options to choose from here."

"Perhaps Mr. Cooper would like to try some?" Brenda tried to hide the disappointment in her voice as she held the tray through the serving window to the two men. "These ones are baked and these are fried."

"Wow, did you do the decorations on these?" Cooper smiled. "Quite impressive."

"I can make custom designs as well. I love piping different decorations on them."

"What a nice advantage to have. Not only does it smell delicious, but it looks like artwork. All right, I'll try one." Cooper picked up one of the donuts and took a big bite. "Mm, wow, this might be the best donut I've ever tasted, and I like that the glaze isn't overly sweet. It's the perfect combination. I'm surprised I haven't heard of your truck before."

"We're fairly new, we've only been open a short time." Joyce handed him a napkin to go along with his donut. "We'd be happy to cater any event that you might organize."

"I will be keeping you in mind. I could never pass up delicious donuts like these."

"Thank you." Brenda smiled and waved as the two men walked away, then turned to Joyce.

"Great job, Brenda, I think we're on his radar," Joyce said happily.

"I hope so."

Joyce's smile disappeared, replaced by a determined look. "Now, I need to settle things with Gus. If he thinks he can trip you and get away with it…"

"No Joyce, please don't, I don't want to stir up any trouble."

"You could have been hurt, Brenda." Joyce met her eyes. "It's okay to stand up for yourself, or to let someone else stand up for you."

"I know, I know, I just don't want to cause an issue when there really doesn't need to be one. Please?"

"All right, but just know if he does it again, I'm going to make sure that he gets fried right along with those pickles."

"You wouldn't." Brenda laughed.

"I would if it came to it." Joyce raised her fist in the air. "No one messes with my Brenda."

"Aw, how sweet." Brenda grinned. "I'm going to

make another batch of donuts before the crowd gets here."

"All right, I'm going to walk this jacket down to the dry cleaners. The sooner we get it back to Pierce's office, the better."

"Here, let me give you money to cover the cleaning."

"No, not a chance. Consider it a business expense. I'll be back in a little while."

Joyce headed off in the direction of the strip of stores that lined the street. Green Street was the center of the food truck owners' world. It was zoned for street sales, and it was the only place in the city that they were approved to congregate all year round. Situated between several streets of office buildings and a high school as well as being close to some tourist attractions, it was a prime location. Joyce walked past a shop that was being renovated. The drilling going on inside drew her attention. She looked inside and realized that they were installing kitchen equipment. She walked past and pushed open the door of 'May's Dry Cleaners' and stepped inside.

"May? May, are you in?" Joyce called out.

"I'm here!" A woman stepped up to the counter

from a back room and smiled. "How did it go? Did you win Pierce and his friend over?"

"Not exactly. This is Pierce's jacket." She held up the suit jacket covered in glaze. "Do you think you can save it?"

"Can I save it?" May shook out the suit jacket and smiled. "Of course I can. I can work miracles behind this counter. But I'd love to hear the story of how this happened."

"I'll tell you the story another time, I promise, but right now I need this jacket cleaned as soon as possible. I'll pay extra for the rush."

"Don't worry about that, Joyce, no extra charge for you. It should be ready in about an hour."

"Thank you so much, May, I'll be back then to pick it up." She turned towards the door.

"I'll bring you some donuts!"

"Yum! Please do!"

Joyce waved as she stepped out of the shop. As she did, a flash of light caused her to squint and look away for a moment. When she looked back, it was gone. She made her way back to the food trucks. As she did, she noticed the 'Donuts on the Move' sign on the donut truck flapping in the wind. It was definitely time to hire the artist and get the sign painted on the side of the truck. She began to visualize the image when her foot caught on something. Her mind spun as she lost her balance and tumbled forward.

"Gus! Not again!" she groaned as her knees and palms hit the ground. With an angry glare, she looked up, expecting to see Gus, but there was no one in sight. Confused, she looked back at her foot, which was still tucked behind a shoe. A shoe that was connected to a leg that disappeared behind the hot dog truck. Her heart raced as she got to her feet and walked around the back of the truck. There, sprawled out on the ground, was Adam. The scream that escaped her throat was piercing even to her own ears, but she couldn't stop it. Adam was dead. It looked like he'd been struck with something on the back of his head.

CHAPTER 3

*J*oyce's high-pitched scream summoned others, including Brenda.

"Joyce, what is it? What's wrong?" Brenda ran up behind her and gasped as she caught sight of Adam. "Oh no!" She wrapped her arms around Joyce and turned her away from the sight of Adam's body. "Are you okay? Did you see what happened?"

"No, I didn't see anything. Nothing. I tripped over him." She sniffled. "How terrible is that? I didn't even notice that he was there."

"It's not terrible, it could have happened to anyone."

"You're right, Brenda, but I still feel horrible about it." Joyce shook her head.

Sirens filled the air as police arrived. Brenda clung to Joyce's hand and guided her to a bench not far from their truck. She'd never seen Joyce look so pale. "Are you sure you're okay? That must have been quite a shock."

"Yes, I'm okay, of course I'm okay, I'm not the one lying on the ground, am I?" Joyce answered sharply.

"I'm sorry." Brenda bit into her bottom lip.

"No, I'm sorry." Joyce sighed. "I didn't mean to snap at you. I just feel so guilty. I don't know why. We just saw him not twenty minutes ago, how can he be dead?"

"I don't know, but from the look of it, it was no accident. Someone attacked him." Brenda shivered at the thought. "I didn't hear anything, but I was busy with the donuts. I had music playing and there was music playing from some of the other trucks and some noise from the shop they are renovating, so maybe that's why I didn't hear anything. I don't know what to think. How is it possible that someone could be murdered one truck away, and no one saw or heard anything?"

"That's what I'd like to know." A police officer paused beside them. He reached up and took off his hat. "I'm Officer Reynolds." He looked between the two women. "Which one of you found the body?"

"I did." Joyce frowned. The man seemed quite young, much younger even than Brenda. "I just stumbled over him, quite literally. Do you have anything to go on?"

The officer shook his head. "Not just yet, there are no cameras near where the body was found, but I'm looking into getting the camera feeds from the local stores. First, I want to speak with any witnesses. As of now, you seem to be the only ones that were anywhere near Adam when he was killed."

"We just saw him about twenty minutes before he was found, so whatever happened to him, it happened pretty recently," Brenda explained. "I didn't hear or see anything until Joyce screamed."

"And what exactly did you see?" The officer turned to face Joyce.

"You know what I saw, I mean it's the same thing that you've seen. I'd rather not go into detail about it." Joyce shook her head. "It's horrible."

"Yes, I know it is. I'm sure that you are in shock, but any small detail could be helpful. Since the murder took place so recently, it's possible that you witnessed something and just didn't realize what it was."

"I was at the cleaners. I left and walked back towards the truck, and then I tripped over Adam. It's that simple. There was nothing else to see," Joyce explained.

"What about while you were in the cleaners?" The officer looked at her intently. "Did you notice anyone in there with you? Maybe someone that left right as you came in?"

"No, it was just May, the owner. She was in the back and came out front when I walked in. She wouldn't have been in the back if there were any other customers inside."

"Did you notice anyone walk past the window? Someone on the sidewalk? Did you hear any sounds, an argument, shouts?"

"No, there was no one, and no, I didn't hear anything. I'm sorry, I really wish I could help, but I honestly didn't see anything."

"It's all right, I understand. The detective on the case is probably going to want to speak with you when he arrives. If you think of anything at all, please call this number right away." He handed her a business card. "The sooner we find any kind of evidence, the better chance we have of solving this case."

"Yes, of course. We'll do that." Joyce tucked the card into her purse.

"Please exercise caution. We're warning everyone in the area, as at this time we have a murder and no suspect, which puts everyone at risk."

"Yes, of course we will." Brenda met the officer's eyes. "Anything we can do to help, we'll be sure to call you."

As he walked away, Joyce stepped closer to Brenda.

"All of this is very strange. I don't think Adam was killed for a random reason. He's right, we really do need to be extra cautious."

"I'll keep that in mind," Brenda said.

As soon as the police gave permission for the witnesses to leave, Brenda headed for her car. When she noticed that Joyce stayed beside the truck, she paused and looked back.

"Aren't you going home?"

"No, I think I'll stay for a little while. I want to keep an eye on things."

"Do you want me to stay, too?" Brenda asked.

"No, go home to your family, make sure that

they know you're okay. I'll see you tomorrow morning." Joyce pointed towards Brenda's car.

"Okay." Brenda frowned. "I don't like the idea of leaving you here alone though."

"Don't you start treating me like an old lady. I am just fine by myself."

"Okay, I'll see you tomorrow, Joyce." She gave her friend a quick hug.

"Tomorrow." Joyce nodded as tears filled her eyes. Living alone, she rarely had the comfort of someone else's arms around her. It still startled her when Brenda would hug her, but in a pleasant way. However, in that moment, the hug revealed just how bothered by Adam's death she was as tears sprung to her eyes. With no one to go home to, she thought it best to stay for a bit and see if she could find out what some of the truck owners thought about Adam's murder. It didn't take long to start hearing their opinion on things. Matt, who ran the pizza truck, made his way over to her. He shoved his hands in his pockets as he reached her.

"You doing all right, Joyce?"

"I guess." She frowned. "It's a sad day."

"Yes, it is. I'm still having a hard time believing that it happened. And to Adam. He was a good kid."

"Yes, he was, from what I knew of him. Did you know him well?" She peered at him for a moment.

"We hung out a few times. He was involved with some people that weren't my speed." He pursed his lips.

"What do you mean by that?" Joyce's eyes widened.

"He's about ten years younger than me, so it figures, but the crowd he hung out with was too reckless for me. Always getting drunk, getting into trouble. Adam tried to keep them in line, but I could tell that even he thought they were out of control sometimes."

"Why do you think he continued to spend time with them?" Joyce asked.

"They were friends from high school, he said. But it was more than that. He treated them like family, as if he couldn't do anything but accept them. I didn't really understand it." Matt shook his head. "I tried to advise him to give himself some space from those types, but he refused. He wouldn't tell me why."

"Do you think they might have had something to do with this?"

"I don't know. I doubt it, considering how close they were, but really, anything is possible."

"Do you know any of their names?"

"Just first names, and even those might have been nicknames."

"Did you mention them to the police?"

"I didn't really think of it." He frowned.

"I would consider it. You knew Adam better than me, you might know something that could help the case."

"I'll mention it to them." He nodded. "How are you holding up?"

"I'm okay, Matt, thanks for asking."

"Do you want a ride home or something?"

"No, I'm fine really. I just need a chance to calm my nerves."

"Coffee?" He smiled.

"No thanks, I'm not sure that would help." She offered a smile in return.

After Matt walked away, Joyce noticed that most of the other truck owners were leaving as well. It might seem strange that she lingered, but something was bothering her deep inside. She didn't believe that someone could kill a man only a few feet from other people and not leave behind a clue as to what happened. What made her feel even worse was that she was certain that she was likely the best witness available. Yet, all she could recall was walking to the cleaners, then tripping over Adam's body. There had to be something that she missed.

She walked the distance from the truck to the cleaners again. May's sign was turned to closed, as were most of the shops on the strip. The owners knew that they wouldn't get much traffic with part of the street being a crime scene. When she turned back to face the row of trucks, she noticed that the view was clear. All at once, she remembered the flash that she'd seen as she stepped out of the cleaners. It wasn't normally there, and it had startled her. Her heart raced as she wondered if she might have seen more than she realized. But what could a flash have to do with the murder?

CHAPTER 4

*B*renda pulled into the driveway of her three-bedroom home and stopped to take a breath before she turned off the car. Normally, she would head straight for the door, eager to see her husband and daughter. Today, she needed a few minutes to gather her thoughts. Breaking out into her own business had been a bit of an issue between herself and her husband. He had images of her being a homemaker, while she was too restless to settle into that role. She began baking cakes and treats for all of the local bake sales. Her baked goods became so popular that people would pay her to make treats for parties. Word got around about the delicious morsels she created. Joyce heard about it and purchased some cakes from a bake sale, then had shown up at her door one day and asked her to make some more. Even though it wasn't an official business, Brenda was proud of what she'd been able to do.

When Joyce offered her the opportunity to run the truck together, Brenda jumped at the chance. Her husband was less enthusiastic. Though their daughter was in school, he sometimes worried about Brenda working outside the home. Because of his job as a journalist, he heard a lot of bad news, which made him concerned at times for Brenda and Sophie's safety. Brenda convinced him with statistics about the safety of the area and how much it fulfilled her. However, that would change the moment he found out about the murder. She guessed he would be pretty upset. Still, she had to tell him.

Brenda stepped out of the car and started walking towards the door. She opened it to see Charlie standing at the end of the hallway.

"Brenda? Are you okay?" He rushed towards her as she closed the door behind her. "I just heard about what happened, why didn't you call me?"

"I'm sorry, hon, I was a little caught up with

things. Joyce is the one who found Adam, and she was a bit upset."

"I understand that. I'm upset, too." He frowned and wrapped his arms around her. "I was upset from the moment that I heard about it. I didn't know what to think."

"I'm sorry, I should have called you. I honestly didn't think that word would get around so fast. Is it already on the news?"

"Yes, it is. They even showed the trucks. I had to turn it off because Sophie recognized the donut truck."

"Oh no, I didn't even think of that. Where is she?"

"Having a tea party in her room. Don't worry, she didn't hear what happened."

"I should go to her." Brenda started to turn away.

"Wait." He looked into her eyes. "Are you okay? Really?"

"Yes." She nodded. "It's honestly hard to believe."

"I thought you said that this was a safe area?"

"It is, you looked into it yourself, you know it is." She frowned.

"I know I did." He sighed and took her hands in

his. "I don't mean to upset you more, I really don't. I just can't stop thinking about how it could have just as easily been you. Isn't his truck right next to yours?"

"Yes, it is, but…"

"One truck away, Brenda. One truck away." Charlie looked at her with desperation.

"Don't worry." She took his hand. "Adam was killed for a reason that had nothing to do with me. I wasn't the target, and I don't think it was random."

"Do you know what the reason is? Do the police know who killed him?"

"I'm not sure. We'll find out the truth soon enough. But I don't think that it was random. Someone targeted him, and there is no reason for anyone to target me or Joyce."

"How can you know that? Maybe it was a crime of opportunity. Maybe someone was looking for a victim and he was available, just as easily as you could have been available."

"Maybe, but I'm okay. I should have called you and let you know what was going on. I'm sorry for that. I was just so focused on making sure that Joyce was okay, it slipped my mind."

"It's all right, I understand. How is she holding up?"

"Okay, I think. I tried to get her to come home with me, but she wouldn't have it. She said she had some other things she wanted to look into."

"Sit down and rest. Do you want me to get you some coffee?"

"No, I'm probably better off sticking to water right now. I'm still a little jumpy."

"I'll get you some water." He disappeared for a moment as she settled on the couch. When he returned, he had the water as promised. After handing it to her, he sat down beside her. "What's Joyce's plan? Is she going to close the truck for a while?" he asked hopefully.

"No, I don't think so. I think she's planning to open tomorrow morning."

"Wow, don't you think that's a little fast?"

"It's important not to look like we're intimidated by what happened."

"But it will help keep you safe and prevent you from getting thrust into the middle of an active investigation."

"And if they don't solve it, how long would we have to remain closed?"

"I don't know." He met her eyes.

"We can't close the business indefinitely." She

kissed him, then settled back against the couch. "I'm just exhausted."

"You rest." He stood up and grabbed a blanket from the linen closet. By the time he returned, she was already stretched out on the couch. He draped the blanket over her. As she closed her eyes, she thought about Joyce and what she might be up to. Was she trying to find out more about the murder?

~

Joyce stood in front of her refrigerator and stared at the assortment of healthy food. She'd become determined to live more healthily and went on a health food shopping spree. After the morning's events, she wished she could find something other than fruit and vegetables. A brownie would be nice. With a sigh, she closed the door and turned to find Molly behind her.

"Hi sweetie." She picked her up and carried her to the couch. "I've had a very rough day. I'm so glad you're here to snuggle with." She patted the top of the bunny's head. "I still keep thinking about what might have happened if I'd left the cleaners sooner. Maybe I would have interrupted the killer, and Adam would still be alive." She closed her eyes and pictured Adam the last time she saw him. To her, he was just a kid, just starting out in life and happy. She considered the conversation she'd witnessed the night before and wondered if it might have had something to do with what happened to Adam. Maybe he tried to double-cross Vince, or cheat him somehow. As much as she didn't want drugs to be in the area, she didn't want a murderer on the loose either. After she watched a show with Molly, she retired to her room. Even after a bath and changing into pajamas, she couldn't relax. She paced back and forth, not unlike Davey once did when he had trouble with a case.

"I know I should stay out of it, I know the police will handle it, but how can I risk the truck and everything Brenda and I have invested in it?" She paused right in front of her husband's picture and frowned. "You wouldn't let things rest, would you? Nope, like a dog with a bone, you would chew this to bits." She sat down on the edge of the bed and took a deep breath. There were times when she missed her husband deeply, but in many ways she didn't consider him to be gone. His memory was still so alive in her mind that just an imagined conversation could give her comfort. "Yes, you're right, Davey. Things can't just be ignored or swept under a rug. Where there's a bad apple, there's bound to be a bad bushel." When she was finally able to fall asleep, her mind still swirled with ideas of how to solve the crime herself.

As Joyce slept, strange images filled her dreams. The dream itself was fractured into bits and pieces. At one point she saw Adam waving to her from his truck, but a bright flash of light blinded her, and when her eyes opened again she saw a wide open meadow, silent and without a soul in sight. At another point in the dream Brenda and her daughter Sophie walked down the sidewalk towards the donut truck. She felt desperate to warn them about something, but no matter how fast she ran, she couldn't catch up with them. She tried to yell to get their attention, but not a sound escaped her lips. Just as Brenda began to look over her shoulder, another flash of light blinded her. When she opened her eyes again, Davey was there, with his endless smile and deep brown eyes. He laughed for no apparent reason. His laughter had always been infectious, and even when she didn't know the joke, she found herself laughing with him. He reached out and wrapped an arm around her shoulders, then kissed her cheek.

"It isn't about the hot dogs, love."

Joyce bolted upright in her bed and drew in a deep breath. Her body was coated in sweat, but her lips were curved in a smile, as if she had just been laughing in her sleep. The turmoil of her emotions was enough to spark a sense of urgency within her. Was there something about the dream that she should remember? If there was, it had faded too fast for her to grasp it. Light already peeked through the window in her bedroom. She glanced at her bedside clock and saw that it was about fifteen minutes earlier than when she would normally wake up.

After a few more moments thinking about the strange dream, Joyce climbed out of bed. Her eyes watered with pain for a moment as her joints protested. Over the past five years, she'd found that mornings became more and more difficult for her, which was one of the main reasons she took it slow. She dropped some extra hay in Molly's bowl, then turned on the coffee pot. The rabbit sniffed and nibbled at her toes.

"Yes, I know, they're cold." She laughed and scooped up the rabbit for a snuggle. After she set her back down, she headed for the shower. Warm water did help to ease some of the stiffness in her body, and usually by the time she finished her coffee, she was in top shape. Mornings were a not-so-gentle reminder that things had changed. She wasn't as spry as she once was. She liked to think she made up for it with the wisdom she'd gained from years of experience.

After Joyce stepped out of the shower and dressed, she and Molly settled on the couch with her coffee and the rabbit's favorite chew stick. It was their morning ritual, and it normally filled her with a sense of peace. But that morning it was weighed down by thoughts of what she might find when she arrived at the food truck. Sure, she could have closed it for the day, and she didn't expect too many customers, but she hoped that she might learn more about what happened to Adam. The flash she'd seen had been repeated in her dreams.

Maybe if she could pinpoint what made it, she could figure something out about Adam's death. Just as Davey always told her, when there was a crime, it didn't matter who the lead investigator was, all that mattered was solving it. He never let his role in an investigation limit him. Sometimes that upset his superiors, and sometimes they applauded him for it. She always felt a sense of pride when he solved a case, not because he got acclaim for it, but because she knew just how hard he worked to do it.

"Now it's my turn, Davey." She smiled at the

memory of him. "Let's see if I can do the same as you."

As she left for the food truck, she double-checked to make sure the door was locked, just as Davey always reminded her, then headed off.

CHAPTER 5

*B*renda sat in her car in the parking lot. She stared at the line of trucks. It was hard to think of going to work without Adam being there to greet her. She'd never really thought about what an impact he had on her day. He always had a smile and a wave for her, and even though they didn't know each other well, his good attitude tended to put her in a better space no matter what happened in the morning.

Since she worked most of her hours on the weekends, it was generally pretty easy to get out the door. But on the weekday mornings that she worked, it could be very chaotic. Between getting Sophie up and her stuff ready for school, which always included missing socks, missing hair bows, or missing homework, and getting Charlie pulled out of whatever story he was working on long enough to remember to take Sophie to school, by the time she left, she was exhausted. That morning had been even worse, as Brenda was weighed down by thoughts of Adam's murder.

As Brenda stepped out of the car, she tried to focus her thoughts on work so that she wouldn't be distracted by the chaotic morning. On her way to the truck, she noticed that the police line had already been taken down. She guessed that Pierce had something to do with that. He wouldn't want a street that was popular and made the city a decent amount of money to be closed for too long.

Brenda paused beside the donut truck and took in the sight of Adam's hot dog truck. He'd painted it red and tan to depict the hot dogs he sold. It looked so strange as it stood there empty. She guessed that the police had already searched it from top to bottom, and soon it would be removed from the line. Would Adam's family come to claim it? Did he own it, or lease it? These were things she had no idea about. In fact, she didn't even know if Adam had family. She entered the donut truck and was greeted by the sweet aroma that always lingered between the metal walls. It was normally a comfort, but this morning, she found it was the final straw in an already emotional day. Her eyes teared up, and she felt a sob building in her chest.

"Good morning, sunshine!" Joyce's cheerful voice startled her. Brenda spun around to see the smaller woman mounting the steps. "You beat me here again!"

"Here you are with such a great attitude. I wish I could have that kind of cheerfulness."

"Trust me, I'm not always cheerful. I just wanted to start our day on a high note, but it probably wasn't appropriate, considering." She sighed. "I honestly never know how to handle these kinds of things. At Davey's funeral, I wanted to have lively music and dancing, two things he loved. But the rest of those grieving for him didn't agree." She shrugged as she looked into Brenda's eyes. "I guess everyone faces death differently."

"It isn't just Adam. It's this place. I really would feel more comfortable if the murderer was caught."

"I agree, I will feel much better if the murderer was behind bars and all of this gets settled. If you don't want to be here, Brenda, I will understand, and you are welcome to go home. We can close up for today."

"No, I do want to be here. There's nowhere else I want to be."

"Good. I think we should try to help solve this. I can't just stand around and wait for the police to figure this out. I have to do something. We are the ones who saw Adam last, other than the killer, and we are the ones that know about the conversation between Adam and Vince."

"Which I still think we should talk to the police about."

"I agree, but we have to be careful. If it was Vince that killed Adam, and we let the police know that we witnessed them discussing what we think might be a drug deal, then we could be in danger." Joyce winced as she recalled the urgency she felt in the dream the night before. Though she'd never given much credence to prophetic dreams, she couldn't shake the memory. "I know that's awful to say, but drug dealers can be vicious people."

"You're right. But maybe you can speak to the police on the condition of anonymity."

"Yes, okay. I'll give the officer a call as soon as we open up."

"All right, I'll get started on the baking, you get the register open."

The two women worked silently for a few

moments before a voice from outside the truck startled them both. It was too early for customers, and most of the other truck owners were busy setting up for their day.

"Hello? Is anyone in there?"

"Yes?" Joyce leaned out through the window. "Sorry, we don't have anything ready just yet, but if you want to wait a few minutes, it'll be fresh and delicious."

"Oh, thanks for that, but I'm actually here on another matter. My name is Detective Crackle, and I am here to discuss the death of your colleague."

"Crackle?" Joyce looked at him as she held back a smile. "Is that short for something?"

"No, unfortunately, it's just Crackle." He smiled beneath a bushy brown mustache. "Could I have a few minutes of your time?"

"Of course, what can we help you with?"

"I was informed that you were the person that found Adam. I can see that your truck is positioned right next to his. I believe you will be my best source of information during this investigation. If you're willing to help, that is."

"Of course we are. Right, Brenda?" Joyce cast a glance over her shoulder and nodded to Brenda, who offered a smile to the detective.

"We're all hoping that this gets solved quickly." Brenda wiped her hands clean of dough as she walked towards the window.

"Anything you can remember would be very helpful." He pulled out his notebook. "Let's start with you. Joyce, is it?"

"Yes, it is."

"Joyce is such a beautiful name. It's always been one of my favorites." He chuckled, then cleared his throat. "So you discovered the body. How did that happen?"

"I uh, I tripped over his foot." She frowned and shook her head. "It was terrible."

"I imagine it was, and I'm sorry for that. But what I mean is, what were you doing just before that?"

"Oh, I was leaving the dry cleaners."

"The one right here on the street?"

"Yes, May's place."

"Okay, and while you were inside the cleaners, or when you stepped out, did you see anything?"

"No, nothing. I wish I had." She closed her eyes for a moment and recalled the flash in her dreams. "I did see a flash. I have no idea what that could mean. As I was stepping out of the cleaners, I saw a flash. At the time I just assumed it was something reflecting off one of the trucks, but when I went back to what I thought was the same place after the crime, I didn't see anything flashing. It still could be nothing, I mean, it was just a flash. I didn't see anything else."

"Maybe you saw more than you realized in that flash." He made a note in his notebook. "Can you describe it to me? Was it like a camera flash? Or the flash of a car going by?"

"It sparkled. Similar to when the sun bounces off something reflective."

"Ah, I see, that's very interesting. You say you didn't see it again later?"

"No, but now that I think about it, that makes sense. The sun would have been in a different position at that time."

"I will consider that." He made another note. "Now, did you hear anything at all? Maybe a muffled cry? Loud voices?"

"No, nothing. I've been trying to recall, but nothing. Not an engine, not a shout, no footsteps, nothing."

"What about a crash? Or a thump?"

"No." She sighed. "I'm sorry. I know that if I could remember more, then you might have a lead, but I can't remember what I didn't hear or see."

"I understand. You've been a great help. If you think of anything more, just contact me, all right?"

"Yes, I will." Joyce nodded.

"And Brenda, right?"

"Yes." She smiled.

"You were here in the truck while the murder occurred?"

"Yes, I was."

"And you didn't hear anything either?"

"Sometimes when I bake, I turn on music. It helps me to get into the right frame of mind. After the incident that morning, I needed something to clear my head. So no, unfortunately I didn't hear anything."

"What incident are you referring to?"

"Oh, it has nothing to do with Adam."

"I'd like to hear about it just the same, if you don't mind." His warm smile emerged from beneath his mustache again, just before he smoothed it down with his palm.

"Councilman Pierce visited the street that morning and I made him some donuts. However, when I delivered them to him, I tripped."

"She was tripped." Joyce raised an eyebrow.

"Whatever happened, I smashed the donuts on

the councilman's suit jacket. It was very embarrassing."

"That's why I went to the cleaners, to get his jacket cleaned. But I don't think that has anything to do with what happened to Adam," Joyce added.

"It's important that I get the full picture of the last hours of Adam's life. Anything can be significant if it's paired with evidence of some kind. Who do you believe tripped Brenda?"

"I don't just believe it, I know it. It was Gus. He sells fried everything, except for donuts, and in particular, his specialty is fried pickles. He's the one that tripped Brenda, to make sure that his pickles got all of the attention. I know that sounds ridiculous to you, but the food truck industry is highly competitive. It would not be the first time that someone attempted to sabotage someone else," Joyce explained.

"Did anyone have bad blood with Adam? Maybe someone who was in competition with him?" Detective Crackle asked.

"Adam is actually the only one that sold hot dogs here," Joyce said. "I'm not sure how he managed that, other than maybe his hot dogs were so popular perhaps no one wanted to compete with him. But our truck hasn't been open long. The other vendors have been here a lot longer than us and probably know more about the history between Adam and any other vendors."

"Pete does sell burgers and fries, and they had a friendly taste-off that compared their French fries. Adam won, but Pete didn't seem to have any hard feelings about it. They sell different food items, so I don't think they really considered each other competitors." Brenda frowned. "I don't recall any issues between them."

"I'll look into that. Thank you for the input." Detective Crackle shook their hands. "I want to thank you for your time. You've both been very helpful. If I have any further questions, is it all right if I contact you?"

"Anytime." Brenda nodded.

"Same for me." Joyce glanced past him to the nearly empty street. "I do hope that you can solve this quickly. I don't think anyone will be at ease until the murderer is found."

"Rest assured, I will do my best." As the detective walked away, Brenda leaned close to Joyce.

"We need to tell him the truth about Vince. Now is the best time to do it."

"All right, you're right." Joyce leaned through the window again. "Detective Crackle, why don't you come into the truck for a moment? We have some fresh donuts for you to try."

He paused and looked back over his shoulder. When he caught Joyce's eye, he nodded. A moment later, he ascended the steps and joined the two women in the truck.

"I can only assume there's something you don't want anyone else to overhear?" He looked between them.

"You are correct." Joyce peeked out through the window to be sure there was no one nearby, then turned back to the detective. "Adam had a conversation with a man the night before he was killed. He comes across as quite seedy, and rumors around are that he might be involved in criminal activities, in particular drug dealing."

"What man? Do you know his name?" He whipped out his notepad again. Joyce held her breath. Brenda rested a hand on her back.

"We don't want any trouble. He strikes me as a dangerous man." Brenda frowned.

"So then you know who it is?" Detective Crackle raised his brown eyes to Brenda's. She was startled by the sudden eye contact.

"Yes." She glanced at Joyce, then nodded. "Vince. Vince Marritelli."

"Oh, I know that name." He made a note. "What do you think this conversation was about?"

"I don't know." Joyce crossed her arms. Brenda nudged her foot. "What? I don't. It was only a guess of what they might be saying."

"A guess?" Detective Crackle studied her. "Anything you can provide will be helpful, I'm sure of it."

"I think it might have had something to do with drugs. I hate to think that about Adam, but from what I overheard, there was mention of merchandise and pounds. I just can't think of anything else it might have been about. Honestly, I can't be certain that was what it was regarding, I can only guess."

"I think I would take your guess pretty seriously. This might help us out. Is there any reason you didn't report it to the officer yesterday? I didn't find anything about this in his notes."

"Honestly, I didn't want word getting back to Vince that I mentioned it, and I wasn't sure that it would have any relevance to the case." Joyce met his eyes. "But Adam didn't deserve to die, no matter what he was involved in."

"I see. I'm glad that you're on his side. He doesn't have much family to speak of and most of the people I've interviewed say they knew him, but didn't really know him. It's refreshing to find someone concerned about him." Detective Crackle smiled slightly.

"He didn't have anyone?" Brenda sighed at the thought of such a young man so alone in the world.

"Some distant relatives in another state, but his parents both died young and as far as I can tell, he didn't have any siblings."

"Who is going to arrange the funeral?" Joyce asked.

"An aunt from Florida, but she doesn't sound too thrilled with the idea," Detective Crackle explained.

"Well, if you could give her our number." Joyce handed him a business card. "Whatever we can do to help, we will. I'm sure there are quite a few people around here that would like the chance to honor his memory."

"Wonderful, I'll let her know." He tucked the business card into the breast pocket of his suit jacket. "Thanks for the tip, ladies. I will look into Vince. In the meantime, stay safe."

"We will, thank you." Brenda escorted him to the door and waited until he was clear of the steps before she closed the door. She looked back at Joyce. "That was so kind of you to offer."

"It's the least I could do." She shook her head.

"We can't let this rest, Brenda. We're going to need to keep digging."

"I agree." Brenda pursed her lips as she looked out through the window of the truck. "I wonder how many of these other people might know something that they're afraid to speak up about."

"Some people still adhere to a mind-your-own-business philosophy. I'm glad that we told the detective about Vince. Of course he is the obvious suspect. He's probably involved in crime to begin with. But I wonder why he would take such a big risk. He had to expect that fingers would be pointed in his direction when Adam showed up dead."

"Maybe it wasn't thought out. Maybe he got angry and lost control." Brenda placed a donut tray in the oven and put the donuts from a baking sheet into the deep fryer. She picked up the empty baking sheet. As she moved it towards the sink, a beam of sunlight shone through the window and bounced off the shiny baking sheet.

"Oh! That's it!" Joyce gasped. "That's like the flash I saw. It was just like that."

"Like what?" Brenda looked between the baking sheet and the sun, then back to Joyce.

"I knew it was a reflection of some kind. Oh my, Brenda, what if it was a reflection off the murder weapon? Whoever killed Adam might have swung his weapon through the air and caught the sunlight on its surface."

"If that's the case, then whatever was used to kill Adam must have been metal, or at least made out of something reflective."

"Like a baking sheet? I'm not sure that something like that could do so much damage."

"No, I don't think so either." Brenda picked up the sheet and tapped it on the counter. "It's much too light."

"But I know it was that kind of flash. It was just as bright." Joyce pointed towards the baking sheet. "I think we should test this out."

"How can we do that?" Brenda washed off the baking sheet as she listened to Joyce's idea.

"We can recreate the moment. The scene is no longer roped off, so we can position ourselves the best we can where we think the murderer might have been, at exactly the same time that I saw the flash. Maybe we'll be able to recreate it. If the baking sheet doesn't give the same reflection, then we might be able to try out other things."

"Maybe the police already know what the murder weapon is. That might be an easier way to figure it out," Brenda suggested.

"Yes, it might be. But they might not know exactly what it was, and we're not going to have access to that information unless Detective Crackle decides he wants to be very informative, which I doubt he will."

"Okay, I think it's worth a shot trying to recreate the moment. Maybe if we time it right, we'll get a good result."

"At least it's something that we can try. Meanwhile, I think we should consider whether some of Adam's friends might have been involved. According to Matt, they're a rough group. If he had no close family to speak of, then he might have really clung to them."

"That would make sense." Brenda nodded. "Maybe something happened to create some bad blood between them. Do you have any idea how we can find them?"

"No, unfortunately, Matt didn't know any names." Joyce sighed.

"Maybe I can get Charlie to look into Adam's life a little. He has a nose for following the finances, and finances often lead to other things about a person's life."

"Do you think he'd be willing to?" Joyce's eyes widened.

"Yes, I'm sure he would if I asked. Trust me, he's just as interested in finding the killer as we are." Brenda smiled.

~

That evening when Brenda arrived at home, she found Charlie hard at work in his office. She lingered by the door for a few minutes, as he seemed so engrossed. Sophie waved to her from her bedroom and put a finger to her lips. That meant Dad was working on something big. She bit into her bottom lip and started to back away from the door, but the moment she did, a floorboard creaked beneath her foot. Charlie looked up with wide eyes. His shock faded into a smile when he saw her.

"Hey there, beautiful. I didn't know you were home."

"Sorry, I didn't mean to bother you. It looks like you're working hard on something."

"I am." He gestured for her to step in. "Close the door. I don't want Sophie to overhear too much."

"Okay." Brenda frowned as she closed the door behind her. "What's going on, is it a big story?"

"The biggest." He swiveled in his chair to face her. "Now, don't be upset."

"Upset about what?" She raised an eyebrow. "I'm a little upset now, since you told me not to be."

"I just thought it wouldn't hurt to look into things a little. I thought, just to get an idea of what you were up against. I figure that maybe I should try to find out information about Adam."

"Are you kidding?" She laughed and shook her head.

"Okay, not exactly the response I expected." He pushed his glasses up along his nose and studied her.

"I'm sorry, it's just that I was going to ask you to look into him. That's why I was thinking about interrupting you. Did you find anything?" She looked past him at the monitor.

"A few things. His parents were killed in a car accident when he was just a teen. He lived with an aunt on and off for a few years, but mostly off. She didn't seem to have much of a handle on him. Anyway, the one place he could always be found, according to his social media profiles, was a comic book shop on Dash Avenue."

"A comic book shop? He didn't seem like the type to read comic books."

"It's not your typical comic book shop. The things they sell have darker themes. There appear to be events and activities that are more centered around violence."

"Wow. I can't believe I had no idea that he was involved in all of this." She stared at the images of Adam on the screen in a few promotional pictures for the shop.

"I can't say that he currently was. These are old pictures, and none of the recent events list him as a participant. Still, I think the comic book shop is a good lead if you want to give it to the detective on the case."

"I'm sure he'll come across it on his own." Brenda ran her thumb across her lips, then tapped the screen. "Can you print the address for me?"

"I told you not to touch the screen." He huffed dramatically and tapped a few keys on the keyboard. A moment later, the printer whirred to life. "What are you going to do with it?"

"Oh, I just thought Joyce might want to see it." She plucked the paper from the printer tray.

"Brenda." He caught her around the waist and pulled her down into his lap. She laughed at the sudden transition and his playful nature. "I get the feeling you're not telling me everything." He kissed her cheek. "What's Joyce up to?"

"It's fine, Charlie. She just wants to look into things herself a little. We all want the same thing. To feel safe on Green Street again as soon as possible."

"It wouldn't be safe for you to check out this place on your own. Who knows what kind of people hang out there. All right?" He released her from his lap and met her eyes as she stood up.

"I understand your concern, Charlie. But this is my work, my business, that we're talking about. I've put my heart into this truck, and if we end up not being able to stay in this area for some reason, it will be difficult to set up somewhere else. I just want to know that every stone has been turned over, that's all."

"And what happens if you find something rotten under one of those stones?" He ran his hand across his face, then shook his head. "It's a dangerous game to get involved in."

"I'm not getting involved. Just looking from the outside. That's all."

"Okay, but you have to promise me that if you get into any kind of situation that doesn't feel right, you leave, or call me, right away. Can you do that?" Charlie searched her eyes.

"Yes, I can." She stroked her finger along the curve of his cheek. "You know my family comes first, Charlie."

"I do." He kissed her lightly on the lips. "Speaking of family, I might have forgotten to make dinner."

"No problem, I'll whip something up." Brenda smiled.

As soon as she stepped out into the hall, Sophie wrapped her arms around her waist. Brenda took a breath and savored the sweet sensation of her daughter's affection. As much as she wanted to find out who killed Adam, she needed to tread carefully because she didn't want to end up in danger, and like she told Charlie, her family did always come first.

CHAPTER 6

The next morning, Joyce arrived before Brenda for once. She hurried to get to the truck as she had received a text from Brenda that she was running late. Joyce got the oven warmed up, then set an alarm for the time she thought she'd stepped out of the cleaners. She wanted to do her best to recreate the flash.

"Morning Joyce." Brenda stepped into the truck with a smile. "Sorry, I'm running a little behind today. Charlie was able to come up with some information, so we might be able to contact Adam's friends." She held out the piece of paper for Joyce to look over.

"So, this was his hangout?"

"As of a year ago, yes. Charlie couldn't be sure if

he still spent time there, but I would guess that he did, since he'd been going there for so long. Maybe we can check it out after closing?"

"Sounds good to me. But first I want to see if we can make that flash again."

"Absolutely." Brenda immersed herself in baking while Joyce did some research about the comic book shop on her tablet. Not long after, they were flooded with customers.

When there was a break in the rush, Joyce peered out through the window and saw another crowd approaching. "I think they must be here to try to get a look at the crime scene. We're never this busy this early."

"I think you're right. I guess once word got around about the murder, people got curious." Brenda frowned as she washed her hands. "I don't see why anyone would want to have a look, but I guess to each their own."

"It might be a bit like what we're doing. Investigating the crime ourselves. People around here want to feel safe again. Maybe they think by taking a look, they will be able to calm their nerves."

"Maybe." Brenda started a batch of baked donuts as they were quite popular with the afternoon crowd. "Is it time yet?"

"About forty minutes." Joyce peered through the window to see that the sky was still clear. She was relieved to see that it was. It was getting closer to lunchtime, and she could see that Pete's hamburger truck already had quite a queue of people waiting to be served. With the hot dog truck out of commission, his sales had to have doubled.

"Great, these should be ready by then."

"We can close up for a few minutes." Joyce began to sort through the pans in one of the storage drawers. She selected a thick, shiny metal baking sheet, a large, heavy-based saucepan, and a sheet cake pan. The only one she thought could deliver a hard enough blow to harm someone was the heavy-based saucepan, but she doubted that would create the flash she'd seen.

After everything was gathered and the donuts were in the oven, Brenda stepped out to make a call to her husband. While she was gone, Joyce took the time to clean up the counters and wash the dishes. They didn't really have separate tasks, they just did what needed to be done. Aside from the baking, Joyce was involved in every step of the process, and though Brenda tried to show her a few recipes, Joyce always managed to burn things. It was a running joke between herself and her late husband.

She would cook, and he would scrape the remains out of the pan. For the first ten years of their marriage, she thought he enjoyed things charred as he complimented her so much. It wasn't until he finally admitted that he was only trying to be kind that she took a cooking class. That was a disaster. From then on, her husband took over most of the evening meals while she mastered everything else. Since his passing, she ate mostly fresh food and sandwiches, not much that required the oven to be used. She smiled to herself as she set the last pan down on the rack to dry. He'd been so careful with her feelings, and at the time it infuriated her that he would lie to her. But now, looking back, she understood just how much he valued her.

"Hey! What's burning?" Pete stuck his head through the serving window.

"What?" Joyce sniffed the air and detected burnt donuts. "Oh no!" She lunged for the oven door and reached for the pan.

"Joyce, don't!" Brenda shouted as she rushed into the truck. Joyce froze just before she would have grabbed the hot pan with her bare hands. She took a step back as Brenda moved in front of her with an oven mitt and pulled the pan out of the oven. She set it on the stove and turned off the oven.

As the truck filled with the scent of burnt dough, Joyce leaned back against the counter behind her and tried to calm her breathing. What was she thinking?

"Joyce, are you all right?" Brenda turned to look at her.

"Yes, I'm sorry. I just didn't think about getting the oven mitts." She shook her head. "I should have taken the donuts out of the oven, I'm so sorry."

"No, they still had a few minutes left." Brenda frowned and kicked the side of the oven. "I think this thing is acting up again. We're going to have to have someone look at it."

"I can get you my guy if you want." Pete leaned on the outside of the truck. "He worked on my deep fryer last week."

"Yes, that would be good." Joyce placed a hand on her heart and willed it to slow down. The fact that she'd almost burned her hands still had her a little unsettled.

"Well, these are done for, and I think the pan is, too. I'm going to take it to the dumpster so we can hopefully get this smell out of here. I don't think customers are going to be too interested in buying burnt anything."

"Yes, you're right. I can take it though if you want."

"No, it's all right. When I come back, we can close up and let the place air out a bit while we do that experiment."

"All right, yes, that sounds good." Joyce forced a smile to her lips.

Brenda was too kind to say anything about it, but Joyce could see the worry in her eyes. It wasn't the first time that Joyce had done something absent-minded. On one of the rare occasions she had helped Brenda make the donut dough, she'd poured an entire cup of flour into a mixture that called for sugar. It was just hard for her to keep things straight sometimes as her mind tended to wander on to other topics.

"I'll walk with you." Pete met Brenda at the bottom of the steps.

"Okay, if you'd like." Brenda glanced over at him and noticed that he had ketchup smeared all over the front of his apron. He was one of the messiest people she'd seen on the street. Somehow, by the end of the night, he always had every possible condiment on his apron, and other areas of his body, including his hair. In his forties, Pete had a dark and steamy look that made him fairly attractive. Many of the women that worked in the trucks, and the customers who visited, would go out of their way to talk with him. Brenda, on the other hand, found him to be a bit arrogant, and since she had no interest in anyone other than Charlie, his handsomeness was lost on her.

"So, any news about Adam?" Pete asked.

"No. You could call and check with the detective if you want." She headed straight for the dumpster.

"No, I'd rather not. You know, once you get too involved, they're going to find something they don't like."

"Oh, I don't know if I would say that." She smiled and opened the lid to the dumpster. "As long as you don't have anything to hide, I'm sure you'll be just fine."

"Who doesn't have something to hide?" He chuckled. "We all have a past, am I right?"

She tossed the donut pan into the dumpster, then turned to look at him. "I'm not sure. I don't think I have anything to worry about in my past."

"Oh no? I guess you're one of the few."

"How are you handling the increase in business?"

"It's great. I mean, not that Adam is dead, but it's nice to have so many customers. I'm sure they will get a new hot dog guy in eventually. Too bad, because I really liked Adam. No one can replace him."

"You're right, things aren't going to be the same at all. I'm still having a hard time even looking at his truck." Brenda frowned.

"Don't worry, you won't be looking at it much longer. They're going to pull it out of here tonight."

"Wow, so soon?"

"I think whatever relative he had is trying to sell it. I guess it's a good idea to get it away from where he was killed. Maybe she'll get better money for it that way."

"Maybe." Brenda turned and started walking back towards the truck. Pete started to follow after her but got distracted by Matt. She was relieved and quickened her step to get back to Joyce. When she stepped into the truck, she was hit with the scent of the burnt donuts.

"Ugh, who knew dough could turn so ugly." She stuck out her tongue.

"My thoughts exactly." Joyce winced. "Let's leave all of the windows open."

Once the truck was as opened up as it could be, they each took a handful of pans and headed down the steps.

"Pete told me they're going to be pulling Adam's truck tonight." Brenda glanced around, then looked back at Joyce. "Do you think we should see if we can take a look around inside before they do?"

"Good thought. Yes. But how are we going to get in?"

"I'm not sure. Did anyone else ever open up for Adam? Some of the other vendors do that now and then if they expect a delivery and they aren't going to be around."

"Maybe Matt?" Joyce raised an eyebrow.

"Yes, maybe. Let's ask him about it later. Right now we have to get to that spot and see if we can figure out our flash." Brenda nodded.

Joyce made her way carefully down the steps with her arms full. When she reached the bottom, she made her way towards May's shop. For the first time, she noticed that it was still closed. "Wow, I wonder why May isn't open? That's not like her. She hasn't closed once since we've been here. I still have to get Pierce's suit jacket back."

"Maybe she was shaken up by what happened." Brenda tilted her head towards the line of shops. "A few people didn't open up today."

"Yes, I guess you're right. I'll make sure to check on her when she opens again. Here." Joyce paused a few steps from the door of the cleaners. "This is where I stood."

"Okay, I know the area where Adam was, so let me walk over there." Brenda took the pans with her and paused where she thought Adam's body had been.

"A little more to the right and back, behind the truck. If Adam was on the ground there, then the killer had to be a few steps away."

"Oh, you're right." Brenda nodded and moved into the new position. "How's this?"

"Good." Joyce gave her a thumbs up.

"Here's the first one!" Brenda swung the baking sheet through the air.

"Yes! That's it. Well, not quite. It was a bit brighter."

Brenda went through each of the pans that she had. Every time she swung one Joyce saw a flash, but it wasn't exactly what she'd seen the day Adam was killed. None of them was bright enough. As she shook her head in reaction to the last one, Brenda walked back towards her.

"Do you want me to go through them again? Maybe the lighting isn't right?"

"No, I don't think it's that. I think it's because we don't have the right murder weapon. No point in trying them again. Besides, I doubt most of the pans would have been strong enough to kill him. But after this, I am almost certain that the flash I saw was the murder weapon being wielded. That at least puts us one step closer to the killer." Joyce looked over her shoulder at the cleaners, then back again at Adam's truck.

"I'd better go check and see if the smell has cleared out. Are you coming?" Brenda piled up the pans in her arms.

"You go ahead, I'll be there in just a few minutes. I want to see if there's anything I missed."

"All right. Don't stress yourself out too much. I'm sure if there was anything here to find, the police would have found it." Brenda walked back towards the truck.

Joyce walked the path to the cleaners and back again. Then for a third time. She observed everything around her. Was there a camera nearby? A surface where she might have seen a reflection without realizing it?

On her way back for the third time, she saw May opening the shop.

"May." Joyce waved.

"Joyce." She turned to look at her. "How are you? It's just terrible what happened to Adam."

"Yes, I know. I wanted to check on you. It's unlike you to be closed."

"Oh, I wasn't going to open today given what happened, but I decided that it's better to get on with business as usual."

"That's the way I feel, too." Joyce smiled slightly.

"But I must be honest, I got a very good offer from a buyer to sell the shop just last week, and I turned him down." May sighed.

"Really?" Joyce's eyes widened.

"I am reconsidering that decision now, though."

"Don't make any rash decisions. Let things calm down a bit."

"I will, but it's just so upsetting."

"It is." Joyce nodded.

"The jacket you brought in is ready. Would you like to pick it up now?"

"Yes please." Joyce followed her into the shop.

Once Joyce had the jacket, she walked out of the dry cleaners and began to walk the path back to the truck. As she did, she noticed a delivery van pull up to the hot dog truck. Her heart lurched as she realized that no one had canceled Adam's deliveries. She walked over to inform the driver, but before she could reach him, the van pulled away. Beside the door of Adam's truck was a stack of paper sealed in plastic. On closer inspection, she saw that they were menus for his truck. Most of the trucks had them to hand out to customers, especially for catering jobs, and they also delivered them to the surrounding office blocks. Joyce thought the timing was unusual since menus were usually ordered in January when prices were increased.

Unless he had run out early or made a change to his menu, there was no reason for him to order more. Joyce peered through the plastic and discovered that one of the menus was face up. It showed his usual assortment of hot dogs and condiments, but there was also a new section that included hamburgers. It surprised her to see it, because as far as she knew, Adam had never sold hamburgers before.

Using her fingernail, she cut into the plastic just enough to slide out one of the menus. She was certain that it wouldn't be missed. Still, she cast a guilty glance around to be sure no one was watching. When she opened the menu, she found that Adam had an entire list of various burgers for sale. Her first thought was about Pete, the hamburger truck owner. Did he know that Adam was going to start selling hamburgers? She doubted he would have been happy about it. She tucked the menu into her pocket, then crossed the short distance to her truck. Matt stood in front of the serving window. He laughed at something that Brenda said.

"Matt, just who I wanted to see." Joyce paused beside him. "Did you know that Adam was going to add hamburgers to his menu?"

"He was? No, I didn't know anything about that. Pete wouldn't be happy about it." He frowned and looked down the line of trucks to Pete's. "I guess there's no point in telling him now."

"No, probably not. Listen, I loaned Adam two bowls a few days ago. I heard that his truck is going to be removed tonight. Do you by any chance have a key so I can get inside and take a look around for them?"

"Oh sure, I have one." He reached into his pocket and pulled out his keys. After fumbling through the large number on the key ring, he selected one. Joyce handed Brenda the jacket and followed Matt as he walked over to Adam's truck. "I haven't been in there since. I know there are things I could box up, to help out his aunt, but I just couldn't bring myself to do it. I even got some boxes." He pointed to a stack of boxes beside the truck.

"I can take care of that. Don't worry." Joyce patted his shoulder.

"You can? Thanks." He smiled with relief as he unlocked the door to the truck and then stepped back. "Anything perishable has already been removed, but everything else besides what the police took is still in here."

"Thanks Matt, I'll get as much as I can boxed up." Joyce reached down and grabbed a few boxes then stepped onto the truck.

CHAPTER 7

*O*nce the door to Adam's truck swung shut behind Joyce, she began to look around the interior. She'd never actually been inside his truck. The décor was typical of a young single man, with a few posters of rock bands and a wall of pinned-up photos. She paused in front of the pictures and looked through them. Since she didn't know who most of the people were, she took a few photographs of them to look through later. Many were of Adam and the same three or four people about his age. A few were of him and Matt. She took those down and tucked them into her pocket to pass on to Matt. She noticed a small passport-size photo of a lady behind one of Adam's photos, so she took a photo of that as well. There were traces of fingerprint powder on the counters, the only indication that the truck had been searched and processed.

As Joyce looked through the inventory on the shelves, she noticed that there were hamburger wrappers. He'd certainly decided to add them to his menu. When she walked past the hot dog bins, the smell of them drew her attention. They'd been emptied, but there was still a lingering scent. She reached for a lid and put it on one of the bins. When she reached for the other, she didn't find it. After looking through the entire truck, she realized that it wasn't there. The other lid was large, shiny, and made of a thick metal. It had enough weight to do some damage if it was swung through the air. She snapped a picture of the remaining lid, then set about packing boxes.

As Joyce sorted through paperwork and piles of unopened mail, she discovered a small brown package. It had the return address of the comic book store. The top of the package was slit open, as if someone took a look inside without opening the entire package. She peered through the opening and saw there was a framed photograph inside. It showed Adam, with the comic book store's sign right behind him. He obviously spent a lot of time at the store. She placed the package into one of the boxes, then finished gathering most of the rest. By the time she was done, she was a little winded. She stepped down out of the truck to find Brenda nearby.

"I was just coming to check on you. You've been in there for a long time."

"I know. I got caught up in boxing everything up, I didn't realize how long I was gone. I hope you weren't too busy."

"No, it's been pretty quiet this afternoon. I'm not sure it's even worth it to stay open at this point. A few of the other trucks are closing up."

"What about Pete's?" She locked the door and tucked the keys into her pocket along with the pictures she intended to give to Matt.

"He is still open. He's getting most of the customers."

"It looks like Adam was going to be selling hamburgers for sure. I wonder if Pete knew about it."

"If he did, he didn't mention anything to anyone from what I can tell." Brenda narrowed her eyes as she looked in the direction of Pete's truck. "Do you think he might have found out?"

"Maybe." Joyce crossed her arms and watched

as Pete handed a hamburger to a customer. "He's a strong man, that's for sure. Much larger than Adam. I think I may have figured out what the murder weapon was."

"You did?" Brenda looked back at her.

"This." She showed her the picture of the lid on her phone. "The other one is missing. It was nowhere in the truck."

"That would mean that whoever killed Adam was probably let onto the truck by Adam or had access to his truck." She frowned and lowered her voice. "The only one we know who has a key is Matt."

"Matt?" Joyce blinked, then looked in the direction of Matt's truck. "I hadn't even considered that. They were friends."

"Friends get upset with each other sometimes." Brenda shook her head. "I don't want to think it either, but it's something we should consider."

"Look at these." She pulled the pictures out of her pocket and held them out to Brenda. "It doesn't look like there's any bad blood between them." One of the pictures showed Matt with his arm around Adam's shoulders. Another was of the two of them fishing.

"No, it doesn't. It looks like Matt was trying to

be the older brother that Adam didn't have." Brenda sighed and handed the picture back. "But things do change, and quickly, sometimes."

"You're right. But it's also possible that Adam invited someone on to his truck that day. Maybe it was someone he trusted, or someone he had a deal with."

"Like Vince." Brenda nodded. "Everything seems to lead back to Vince."

"Unless we're missing what's right in front of our faces." She snapped her fingers. "Adam keeps getting all of the good deals on the street. He's adding hamburgers to his menu, he's stocking new supplies, but his business has been about the same. So where is he getting the money to do that? It's possible that he got a loan, but maybe he got the money from someone else. He doesn't have family besides his aunt, and as far as we can tell, his friends weren't in any position to back him. So who do we know that has the money to do that?"

"I don't know, I guess Pierce, and maybe Cooper."

"Pierce and Cooper." She nodded as a slow smile spread across her lips. "Adam was smart. Maybe he thought if he added hamburgers to his menu, he could take out Pete as competition.

Maybe Cooper or Pierce offered to help him with that by fronting him the money." Joyce sighed with frustration. "But why? What would they get out of that?"

"Maybe one of them was an investor?" Brenda led Joyce back to the truck and stepped inside. "We shouldn't talk about this too much in public. There are ears everywhere. But one thing I've noticed with Charlie's stories is that people with money always want more. Maybe Cooper or Pierce saw an opportunity to make a huge profit off Adam's truck if he was the only truck that offered both hot dogs and hamburgers."

"Maybe. I think it's more likely to be Cooper, he's the businessman."

"That's true."

"Unless maybe we are looking at this wrong. Maybe Adam got the money from somewhere else. Maybe he had another investor. Adam was already getting the majority of the gigs, even those that Pete went after. Maybe he had a deal with Cooper to get all of those gigs."

"You think Adam was bribing Cooper?" Brenda shoved her hands in her pockets. "Is nothing sacred?"

"I think I'm going to drop off the key and photos

to Matt and then pay a visit to Cooper. You go home and spend some extra time with your family."

"Wait, I can go with you. It's better if I do, Joyce." Brenda grabbed her purse from the counter and turned to follow her.

"No, Brenda. It's better if I go alone. I want to see if I can find out if he took bribes. If Cooper is involved in this somehow, I don't want you to be in his line of sight." Joyce straightened the collar of her shirt and pulled her car keys from her pocket. "I'll text you an update as soon as I've talked to him. I'm not even sure that he's going to be willing to see me."

"All right, but if you change your mind, just let me know. I can be there in a few minutes."

"I can handle this, I promise." Joyce gave Brenda a quick hug. "It's best if you go home and see if Charlie dug anything else up for us. Then tonight we can go to the comic book store together to talk to some of Adam's friends. All right?"

"Yes, okay. Here, take some donuts with you. Something sweet can get you through just about any door." She packed up some fresh donuts and handed Joyce the box. "Just be careful." Brenda met her eyes. "Don't take any risks you shouldn't."

"I'll be good." Joyce grinned as she took the

box, then looked back long enough to wink at Brenda.

"See, that right there is what worries me." Brenda sighed and offered a short laugh.

"I'll text." Joyce left the truck with her heart full of determination. She wanted to know just how Cooper was involved in Adam's death, if at all.

~

When Joyce arrived at Cooper's office, she wasn't feeling as confident about her chances of speaking with him. His office was at a large company in a very nice area of town, which meant that he was probably an influential and busy man. Still, she put on her most professional attitude and made her way through the front door. As the receptionist looked up at her with a sour expression, she decided that Brenda was probably right and held out the donuts in front of her.

"A delivery for Melvin Cooper. Does he have a free minute?" Joyce smiled.

"A free minute?" She peeked inside the box and smiled before she looked back at Joyce. "He never has a free minute. But I'll check to see if he wants to speak with you. What was your name?"

"Joyce, from the donut truck."

"Donut truck? Yum!" The receptionist picked up her phone. A minute later, she hung it up and nodded to the door to her right. "Go on in, he is between meetings."

"Thank you." Joyce picked up the box of donuts and opened it. She held it out to the receptionist. "Would you like one?"

"Yes, please." She picked out a donut. Joyce took the donut box and walked over to the heavy wooden door. When she pushed it open, she was greeted by the scent of cigars and leather. The office lived up to its scent, with dark furnishings and an embarrassing amount of leather and wood.

"Joyce." He smiled at her from behind his desk.

"I appreciate you taking the time to meet with me, Melvin, I know you're quite busy."

"I don't mind at all, I really enjoyed that donut, and I see you brought me some other treats today."

"Yes, I thought you might enjoy some more samples of what we have to offer." She smiled. "It's not a bribe, of course."

"Of course." He opened the box and plucked out a donut. "So, what did you want to discuss? Most of the established trucks have already been listed for the main events, for the next few months at least, but I already have you on my list of trucks to tap for child-centered events. However, most of the time the ice cream trucks are preferred, so it might be tough to get you in there."

"Is there anything that I could do to make it a little easier so we can get some events quicker?" She locked eyes with him.

"I'm not sure what you're suggesting."

"Only that if there were certain things that I could do to make our truck move up on the list, I'd like to know, so that I could improve our chances of being selected."

"Ah, I see." He sat back in his chair and folded his hands across his robust stomach. "What did you have in mind?"

"Perhaps we could exclusively advertise your events in our signage and on our menu."

"I don't think that would get me very far. It's very expensive to run these events, and it takes so much of my time. Every little bit helps." He smiled slightly.

"Are you saying a financial contribution would be more likely to get us a good spot?"

"I of course couldn't say that, but when it comes to gifts, my finances can always use a boost. My wife loves to shop." He gestured to a photograph on his desk of a beautiful blonde woman who could have been anywhere from her mid-thirties to late forties. "After I met all of the truck owners, I had to rush off to meet her at the outlets, and we spent hours there burning through my credit card." He rolled his eyes.

"How much financial help are we talking about?" She studied him. If he was telling the truth about the shopping spree, that ruled him out as Adam's killer.

"We're not talking about it at all, actually. Remember?" He looked into her eyes.

"Maybe if I asked some of the other truck owners, they could give me an idea? Who should I talk to?"

"I'm sorry, I don't know what you mean. Perhaps you could do your own research on that. Anyway, I really only had about six or seven minutes, closer to seven really."

"Seven?"

"Yes, that would be good."

"Hundred?" Her eyes widened.

"Hundred?" He shook his head. "I was talking about minutes. I suppose if we were talking about money, it might be hundred." He smiled.

"That seems reasonable. I'm so glad that I came to talk to you. It's tragic what happened to Adam."

"Oh yes, Adam and I spent a lot of time together. He was a good man. Terrible, what happened." He closed his eyes for a moment. "I had a lot of hope for that poor boy."

"Hope?" She leaned a little closer.

"I kind of took him under my wing. I recognized that he had a lot of potential. He had a mind for business. I thought with a little guidance, he could do great things. You know, I have a soft spot for young entrepreneurs."

"That was so kind of you. He must have been thrilled to have a professional on his side."

"I think he was. I had him over for dinner a few times. I wanted him to see what life could offer." He shook his head. "I never expected this, of course."

"No, no one did," Joyce said. "Did you know that Adam was going to add hamburgers to his menu?"

"He was? I had no idea." Melvin's eyes widened, and he shook his head as his phone buzzed. He glanced at his watch. "Sorry, I have another meeting coming in. I'm sure I'll be hearing from you soon, Joyce." He reached his hand across his desk to her. She took his hand in a firm shake. As soon as she released it, she headed for the door. She didn't want to spend a moment longer around him because he seemed untrustworthy, and that put her on edge. As Joyce left his office, her mind reeled. He'd all but confirmed that he accepted bribes, which more than likely meant that he accepted bribes from Adam. That meant they had a business relationship behind closed doors, and if that was the case, then Cooper might have motive to go after Adam.

Although it appeared that Cooper wasn't an honest man, Joyce wasn't convinced that he was a killer, either. He had an alibi. He spoke highly of Adam and had invited him into his home. It was one thing to accept bribes and quite another to commit murder. She shook her head as her mind swirled with thoughts. As soon as she reached the car, she sent Brenda a text.

CHAPTER 8

*B*renda stepped into the house and was greeted by silence. It startled her at first. Usually Sophie was right there to hug her. A glance at her watch showed that Sophie was likely already in bed. Her heart sank a little. Although she liked working with Joyce in the donut truck, sometimes she regretted the time she missed with her daughter.

"Charlie?"

"In here." His voice wafted out from his office. She followed it and found him in front of his computer.

"Are you working on a story?"

"Not exactly. I'm investigating Adam's murder."

"Have you found anything?"

"Nothing specific, just a lot of financial transactions and business dealings that look a little shady. The deeper I get into this, the more concerned I get, Brenda. I wish you and Joyce would stay out of it." He swiveled in his chair to face her. "How far do you and Joyce plan to dig?"

"All we want is a chance to find out what happened to Adam and to make sure that Green Street stays safe. That's what you want too, right?" She pulled up a chair to the computer desk.

"Yes, of course."

"So let's work together on this. You, me, and Joyce. The sooner that we have the murder solved, the sooner we can all relax again. Right?" She smiled as she looked into his eyes. "I think it's kind of fun actually."

"Murder is fun?" He sighed and glanced back at the computer screen.

"No, not murder, of course. But having the chance to work with you on something. I feel like we're on a team, not just a parenting team, but a real team."

"I guess I can see it that way." He tilted his head to the side as he studied her. "You're so gorgeous."

"Ha, right." She shook her head and looked away.

"Yes, I am right." He pulled her chair closer to his. "Stunning, beautiful, and intelligent. I don't know how I ever got so lucky."

"I'm the lucky one." She kissed his cheek. He drew her in for a real kiss, and for just a second she forgot all about Adam and the truck, and even Joyce. She was immersed in his affection, and the reminder of just how much he loved her.

"Mommy! Mommy! There's a monster under my bed!" The shriek shattered the intimate moment. It sent Brenda's heart racing as she jumped up from her chair.

"See?" Charlie looked into her eyes. "I'm not the only one that worries about monsters under the bed."

"I'm on my way, sweetie." Brenda rushed to her daughter's room. Sophie sat up, with red tear-streaked cheeks, and spread her arms wide for her mother's embrace. Brenda scooped her into her lap and held her tight. "You know, there are no monsters under your bed."

"But I heard one. I heard it!" Sophie sniffled.

"Maybe you were dreaming?" Brenda kissed the top of her head.

"Don't worry, Soph, I'll check under the bed, and in the closet, and in every corner." Charlie began to search the room from top to bottom. As Brenda held her daughter close, she could feel her racing heart slowing in her chest. Charlie was calming her down. "There we go, not a monster in sight. I guess maybe there never was one, hmm?" He smiled as he ruffled her blonde hair. "I think Mommy was right."

"You do?" Sophie gazed at him with wide eyes. "But I heard a monster."

"It was probably just a dream, sweetheart." He kissed the tip of her nose. "Can we tuck you back in?"

"Yes." Sophie sighed as she crawled back into bed. "I can't ever get any sleep with these monsters on the loose."

By the time the blanket was pulled up to her chin, she was already starting to drift back off to sleep.

As they slipped out of her room and back into the living room, Brenda felt a sense of relief that Charlie was such a doting father. He always took the time to ensure that Sophie knew she was loved. Once he sat back down at the computer in his office, he turned to look at her.

"All right, we can work on this as a team, as a trio, on one condition."

"What condition is that?" Brenda braced herself for something unreasonable.

"I want to be informed every step of the way. Whatever you two are getting into, I want to know about it. Is that fair?" He held her gaze.

"Yes, that's fair. But Joyce doesn't always tell me what she's up to, so I can't promise that."

"That's fine. Whatever involves you. All right?" Charlie asked.

"It's a deal." She leaned in close and kissed him. She waited for the expected interruption.

"I think she's actually asleep." He smiled against her cheek. "What do you say we take advantage of a little alone time?"

"Oh honey, I would love to. But I have plans to meet with Joyce and check out the comic book shop where Adam spent a lot of his time."

"Great." He rubbed a hand across his forehead. "I guess I can't compete with that."

"It will never be a competition." She placed a light kiss on his lips, then pulled away as her phone buzzed with a text. "It looks like Joyce is on her way to the shop. She found out that Cooper definitely does take bribes, and Adam was probably paying him off."

"See, that's what I mean, Brenda. This could get very shady very fast, and men with money are men with power." He locked eyes with her. "They don't like to be questioned."

"We'll be careful, I promise." She kissed his cheek, then headed out the door.

On her way to the comic book shop, her mind spun with all of the possibilities that the confirmation of the bribery opened up. Could Cooper have killed Adam in order to keep him quiet about the bribes? Was it possible that there were more truck owners involved, and one of them got angry with Adam? If Pierce got wind of the bribery, perhaps he became angry enough to kill? Or was Pierce in on it the entire time? She parked near the comic book shop's entrance and waved to Joyce, who was already waiting on the sidewalk.

"I can't believe Cooper admitted that to you." Brenda shook her head as she joined Joyce.

"It wasn't so much that he admitted it to me as it was that he was prepared to accept a bribe from me. I'm afraid we might have to play along or he may become suspicious."

"Play along? But we don't have extra money."

"Then we'd better get this case solved quickly, hmm?"

"Yes, you're right." Brenda skimmed the front of the comic book shop and grimaced. "I think we're a little past the age limit for this place." She quirked a brow as she watched a few boys who looked no older than sixteen walk through the door.

"That may be true. We can always pretend we're here to buy something for our kids. My son was into comic books for a little while."

"I bet they were nothing like that one." Brenda pointed out a poster on the front window that seemed to depict an alien race and several female zombies.

"Uh, no, at least I hope not." Joyce laughed. "Let's get in there. Hopefully we can find out something about Adam's personal life from the people in here. According to Matt, they were like family."

"And if they weren't?"

"Well, I guess we're about to find out."

"After you, madam." Brenda held the door open for her. Joyce crossed the threshold from a fairly well-lit street into what resembled a cave. Most of the store was dark, with some black lights scattered throughout. A few colored lava lamps were positioned on bookshelves offering just enough of a glow to illuminate the garish and violent images on some of the covers of the comic books. Joyce clutched her purse a little closer and edged her way further into the shop. Brenda followed right behind her.

"This is not what comic book shops were like when I was a kid," Brenda mumbled as she caught sight of a young man peering at her from behind an almost unnoticeable counter.

"I imagine not. But maybe this will work to our advantage. As dark as it is, they might just mistake us for teenagers," Joyce joked. She paused at the end of an aisle and looked up at a montage of photographs, all of which were somehow glowing. Adam was in just about all of them.

"Are you lost?" A tall man dressed in black leather, with long black hair to match, leaned against the wall beside her. When he smiled, his black lipstick cracked enough to reveal red lips beneath.

"No, not lost." Joyce shifted on her heel to face him. "We're here to learn more about Adam."

"Adam?" His smile faded and his eyes narrowed. "How do you know Adam?"

"We work in the food trucks on the same street." Brenda cleared her throat as a few other young men drew close to them. "On Green Street. We're trying to figure out what might have happened to him."

"We know what happened to him. Someone murdered him." He brushed his hair back from his face. "Nothing can be done about that."

"No, it can't." Joyce looked into his heavily mascaraed eyes. "But I imagine you can understand the need for justice."

"Maybe." He nodded to the other men. "Ease off, I think we're scaring the ladies. Don't mind them. They're not dangerous, just bored and obsessively intense."

"Don't worry, I'm not afraid. Actually, it's comforting to me to be in a place that Adam considered to be like home." Joyce smiled.

"It wasn't like his home, it was his home. I'm Patrick. This is Scott and Tray."

"I'm Joyce, and this is Brenda. We own a food truck on Green Street. Adam was very kind to us and helped us when we first started. We were just hoping to be able to pay some of that kindness back. That's why we're here. We want to know more about him, and you, the people he considered to be his family."

"Adam was a good guy. But we weren't on good terms. It's a shame, because our friendship lasted so long. But he didn't want to listen to reason. I warned him about this, he should have listened."

"Warned him about what exactly?" Brenda glanced at the other two men, then turned her attention back to Patrick. "Was there something Adam was involved in that upset you? Or worried you?"

"Adam was always looking for a way to get rich. He didn't care how. It wasn't that he was greedy, it was that he knew what it was like to have nothing. He never wanted to experience that feeling again. So he worked a few angles trying to get a foothold in a higher tax bracket. I warned him that he was playing with fire, people that wanted money out of greed. But he didn't want to listen. He told me that I didn't think big enough and I would always be stuck in this place." He frowned as he glanced around the shop. "I'm not sure what's so bad about this place. It used to be good enough for him."

"Maybe it was the rough behavior?" Joyce suggested.

"Rough behavior?" He smirked. "What do you mean by that?"

"Adam had a friend, Matt. Did you know him?" Joyce asked.

"That old guy, sure." He shrugged.

"He's barely in his forties." Joyce smiled.

"Old." He shrugged again. "He was always attached to Adam. Kept telling him that he had to think about the future, and that he needed to pull away from us. That's what we got into a fight about. Adam started to think he was better than the rest of us, and he needed to be reminded that he wasn't. We're all on equal ground here."

"Maybe Adam found that he got something from Matt that was lacking in his life. Everyone needs that kind of connection." Joyce gazed into his eyes. "No matter how much you think you don't."

"He had that connection here with us. It was his choice to walk away. He even got tangled up with someone who could have been his mother, all because she had deep pockets. He knew better. I don't want to talk about this anymore." He looked past her to Brenda. "You and your friend need to leave, we're closing."

"Wait, Patrick. What woman was he tangled up with?" Joyce asked.

"I don't know. He wouldn't tell us her name. Just said she was the most beautiful woman he'd ever known. I told him he was losing his mind. Now go." He pointed to the door.

"Patrick, please, there's no reason to be upset. I told you, we were friends of Adam's."

"No, you weren't. I was his friend. I was the one that helped him when he needed it. I was the one that knew just how hard he tried to make himself a success. I knew those things about him."

"I'm sure you cared very deeply for him, Patrick. I'm sorry for your loss." Joyce wrapped her arms around him in a warm hug. Patrick's body stiffened in reaction to the touch. A moment later, he relaxed.

"Thank you." He pulled away from her. "If you do find out what happened to Adam, please let me know."

"I will." Joyce gazed into his eyes for a moment, then led Brenda to the door. Once outside, she turned back to look at her friend. "There's another suspect to add to our list."

"Do you really think he could have murdered Adam?" Brenda looked through the tinted window of the comic book shop. "Maybe out of jealousy?"

"Or rage. He feels betrayed by Adam." Joyce shook her head as she walked towards the car. "It looks like Adam was driven by money. That might be the key to finding out who killed him."

"So, you don't think it was Patrick?"

"I don't have a firm opinion on it yet, to be honest. But as of this moment, I don't think we can rule him out. He was obviously very emotionally intertwined with Adam, and I think that counts for a lot."

"Yes, you're right. What about Cooper? If Adam threatened to tell?"

"Cooper has an alibi, he said he was at the shops with his wife. I can try to find out which shops, but at the moment I don't know where they went, so I have no way to confirm it." Joyce shrugged.

"I guess not." Brenda shook her head. "I'll speak to you in the morning."

"Yes. Hopefully, I'll have come up with more ideas by then."

Joyce opened the door to her car and climbed inside. As she pulled away from the comic book shop, she had an uneasy feeling. Though they were either adults or close to it, they seemed like little boys to her, with no one to guide them. She hated the thought of children growing up with no one there for them. Her own children had their own struggles to face, but one thing they never lacked was love. She wondered if Adam found it hard to accept that kind of caring from Matt because he'd gone so long without it.

When she stepped into the house, Molly bounded up to her. She picked up the bunny and rubbed behind her ears as she carried her to the couch.

"What a day, Molly. What a day." She sighed and trailed her fingertips through the rabbit's soft fur. After a few moments, Molly wiggled out of her lap and jumped down to the floor. Joyce picked up her phone and gazed at her son's phone number on the contacts list. Unlike her daughter who she spoke to quite often, it had been some time since she had really spoken to her son. After the funeral, he seemed to keep himself even more busy. Her finger hovered over the dial button, then chose text instead.

Just want to tell you I love you. I hope all is going well.

Joyce sent the text and smiled to herself. Maybe he would read it, and maybe he would reply. But even if he didn't, she would at least know that it was sent. As she went through the routine of making a small meal for herself, she considered what it would be like to live the way Adam did. She guessed there were times when he had no idea where his next meal was coming from. Perhaps he'd slept outside more than once. She imagined that kind of vulnerable life led to abuse and neglect of all kinds. But he'd over-come all of it to start his own business. The thought that he had achieved all of that, then to be murdered, upset her even more. No, she could not let this go. She had to find out the truth. A few seconds later, she received a text in return.

Love you too Mom.

She fell asleep with her heart warmed despite the stress of Adam's murder.

$\mathcal{E}$arly the next morning, Brenda woke up to a buzz on her cell phone. She wiped at her eyes then checked the clock. It wasn't even seven yet, and it was a day off from the truck. With one hand, she reached around the bedside table until she found her phone. She tried to yank it off the charger so she wouldn't have to sit up, but only succeeded in knocking a glass of water over.

"What's that?" Charlie mumbled beside her.

"It's nothing, don't worry about it." She placed a kiss on his cheek, then slipped out of bed. On her days off, she liked to let Charlie sleep in. She handled getting Sophie to school and usually made them a special breakfast to leisurely enjoy together.

Once she was out of the room and in the hallway, she checked her phone. It was a text from Joyce.

When you get up, let me know. I want to do some research on Pierce's connection to Adam. I think there might be something there that will help solve the murder. You're better with this searching stuff so I could really use your help.

Brenda rubbed her eyes again, then sent a text back to Joyce.

I'm up, do you want to come over for breakfast around nine?

She headed to the kitchen to start getting Sophie's breakfast ready. Moments later, she received a text back.

I'll be there! Thanks!

As Brenda woke Sophie, helped her get dressed, and brushed her hair into a tight braid, she couldn't help but savor each moment. She knew it could be a hassle day in and day out to rush around and meet a certain schedule, but she really enjoyed her alone time with Sophie in the morning when she had it. She got all of the latest school gossip, from who liked ponies and who liked cats, to whether or not she remembered to turn in her spelling homework. They would also sing some of their favorite songs together on the drive to school, and Brenda usually sung them again on the way back home. By the time she reached the house, Charlie was up and wandering around the kitchen.

"Hey! No way! It's my turn to make breakfast." Brenda dropped her keys in a dish on the counter and shooed him away from the carton of eggs he'd taken out of the fridge.

"Oh well, I thought you might have other things to do today."

"Actually, I did invite Joyce over to have breakfast with us. I hope you don't mind."

He looked down at his bathrobe and slippers. "I guess I should put on some pants."

"That might be a good idea." She laughed as she gave him a playful swat.

"Pants." He sighed and headed back to the bedroom. She fought off a pang of guilt for interrupting their alone time. It was important to try and find out who killed Adam, and she knew that Charlie agreed with that. As soon as the pancakes and eggs were ready, there was a knock on the door. Brenda opened it to find Joyce on the other side with a notebook, a binder, and a box of pencils in her hands.

"Here, let me take some of that." Brenda

grabbed the binder and pencils. "What's all of this for?"

"I thought we should start a case file."

"Oh?" Brenda smiled.

"Yes, Davey always did. He would have his own personal case files that he kept at home so that he could look through unsolved cases on his off time."

"He was quite dedicated."

"Yes, he was." Joyce stepped inside. "Oh wow, everything smells delicious."

"Just have a seat at the table and I'll bring you a plate. Do you want coffee?"

"Yes please." Joyce sank down in a chair and set the notebook on the table. "I've been up since four making notes in here."

"Oh Joyce, that's not good, you need your sleep."

"I did sleep a little. But I just couldn't get the thoughts out of my head. I figured I might as well put them down on paper."

"Morning, Joyce." Charlie stepped into the kitchen and offered her a warm smile.

"Morning, Charlie. Thank you for letting me borrow your wife this morning."

"Oh, it's fine. I know you two are working hard on this. Just let me know if you need any help. I have some work I can do in my office. Unless you need it?" He glanced at Brenda.

"No, I have my computer we can use in here. But have some breakfast first, hmm?"

"That, I won't turn down." He grinned. As they ate together, they discussed what they thought of the case so far.

"I think Pierce might be the key. He's the one with all of the influence," Joyce said.

"Right, but what does Pierce really have to do with any of it?" Brenda shook her head. "I mean, Vince is the one with the history of violence and crime."

"That's true, and he's still high on my list. But I just can't shake the feeling that Pierce might be hiding something."

"And what about Patrick?" Charlie took a sip of his coffee. "From what Brenda told me, he seemed a little off-balance."

"Maybe. But he cared a lot about Adam. It would take a lot to go from caring to killing. Don't you think?" Joyce finished the last bite of her pancake.

"In some cases. But it depends. Was he really friends with Adam, or was he possessive of Adam? Even if their relationship wasn't romantic, that doesn't mean that he wasn't unnaturally possessive," Charlie said.

"He did seem very put out by the fact that Adam was friendly with Matt." Brenda tapped her fork on her plate. "That could be a sign that his jealousy went past normal into obsession."

"It could be." Joyce nodded.

"But what about Cooper?" Brenda asked. "Cooper pretty much admitted to taking bribes from Adam. I don't think that Cooper would be able to accept bribes without Pierce knowing. If that ever got out, Pierce would be in trouble. Pierce might have even been taking bribes as well."

"That's a good point." Charlie picked up his plate and carried it to the sink. "It's definitely worth investigating. Let me know if you two need anything." After he disappeared into his office, Joyce picked up the remaining plates on the table and carried them to the sink.

"I just have to wonder, did Pete know that Adam was going to sell hamburgers, and would that be enough to inspire him to kill?"

"I'm not sure, it seems like a stretch, but Pete does seem to have quite an edge to him. Let's see if we can find anything on Pierce first. He should be the easiest to research." Brenda wiped off the table, then set her laptop on top of it. Within a few moments, she had it open to a search engine. "Let's just see what Pierce has been up to over the past few months."

Joyce sat down beside her and peered at the screen as Brenda typed on the keyboard. "How do you do that so easily?"

"Here, I can show you a few tricks." Brenda smiled at her, then turned the computer to face her. "Being married to a journalist, I've learned a few things when it comes to research. There are search engines that are better designed for searching for information about people, and there are also specific ways to word things to get all of the most recent political activities. Here we go." She typed in a few more things, then turned the screen back to Joyce. "That looks like a good place to start, right?"

"Absolutely." Joyce skimmed through the options on the list. She clicked on the most recent topic and when it opened, she saw a large photograph of Pierce. He stood in front of a large building located a few streets away from Green Street. "It looks like he was trying to drum up support to get the area rezoned." She narrowed her eyes. "I had no idea he was involved in this."

"Oh? Is it something you've been keeping up with?" Brenda asked.

"Just a little. If it goes through, we won't be able to have the food trucks on Green Street anymore. I figured there wasn't a chance of it happening, but with Pierce's backing, it certainly could." Joyce shook her head.

"What? But that's ridiculous. He just visited us to show us his support. Why would he do that if he's working against us?" Brenda leaned back in her chair. "I know politicians sometimes play both sides, but this seems a little extreme."

"Something isn't right here." She scrolled through the information. "I don't see why Pierce would want to shut us all down. It's the best street possible for making a high income. The public loves having the trucks there. I did my research before we set up shop, and it was the most stable place when it came to sales."

"I can tell you this much, if he is supporting it, then he has some kind of motivation to be doing so. Maybe we can't figure out what that is right now, but there is a reason. There is always a reason."

"Yes, let's see what this next link is." Joyce clicked on another link, and an array of photographs appeared before her. "Wow, here he is with the man who started the push for the rezoning. They're shaking hands, do you see?"

"That's terrible. That man is so shifty." Brenda crossed her arms and stared at the screen. "I wonder how he would like it if we decided to shut down his office." She shook her head. "I guess he wouldn't care, because he would still get his paychecks."

"Yes, you're right about that." Joyce frowned and stood up from the desk. "No matter what we think, he's the one with all of the power. Now with Adam gone, we may lose a lot of our regular customers. He was a huge draw for the area."

"Not to mention that the unsolved murder is going to make people wary of coming to Green Street to eat. Maybe it would be better to find a new location."

"I can start scouting for one." Joyce pulled out her phone. "The only problem is, like I said, we had the best deal on Green Street. Anywhere else is going to cost us a lot more, and we're not going to get nearly the same amount of foot traffic."

"I guess we'll just have to increase our advertising. Where are we at with the truck wrap?"

"I've got Ella set up to come out this Monday."

"Hopefully we'll still be on Green Street." Brenda grimaced.

"Yes, I think we will be. If Pierce is able to get approval for the rezoning, I think it will still take quite some time before it is enforced."

"I wonder if the other truck owners know about this?" Brenda asked.

"Maybe we should tell them?" Joyce met Brenda's eyes. "We could hold a protest. Get the media involved. Make sure that everyone knows what Pierce is actually up to."

"You know what, Joyce?"

"What?" Joyce winced. "Too much?"

"No, it's just perfect!" Brenda stood up from the desk and turned to face her. "It's just what we need. Pierce is trying to slide this through without us noticing. I thought he was up to something. It's time we let him know that we do absolutely notice what he is up to, and we do not agree with it. I think once we inform the other truck owners, they will want to participate as well."

"Not a bad idea at all. I have a mailing list for all of the truck owners on Green Street. I'll send out an email with these links and we'll see what kind of response we get."

"Good idea."

"We should get some supplies to make signs. That will really make Pierce take notice." Joyce pulled out her phone and started to make a list of things they would need.

"I will tell Charlie about it, too. He might be able to pull some strings and get a few reporters to show up for the protest."

"Tell me about what?" Charlie paused at the entrance of the kitchen. "I was just going to get a drink."

"About the protest we're going to hold on Green Street tomorrow."

"A protest? About what?" He grabbed a bottle of water.

"It seems that Pierce has been supporting, and even pushing for, the rezoning of Green Street. If it goes through, food trucks won't be allowed there anymore." Brenda closed her computer. "Joyce and I are going to organize a protest."

"Interesting." He took a sip of water, then pursed his lips. "I've heard about that from someone. There's a lot of money to be gained from the rezoning by the brick and mortar food businesses in that area."

"Well, we're not going to just stand by and let it happen." Joyce frowned. "He was just on Green Street, all smiles and support. What kind of underhanded person is able to pull that off?"

"A well-practiced, deceitful one." Charlie set down his bottle of water. "Just be aware that if you go up against Pierce, things could get messy, very messy."

"Yes, we're aware." Joyce pursed her lips. "If a man can be that duplicitous, he could very likely be a murderer as well."

"Perhaps, but men of his ilk usually hire someone else to do their dirty work. Watch your step. I'll let a few of my colleagues know about the protest. Just email me when you know what time you'll be starting up," Charlie said before he left the room.

"Great, because the responses are pouring in." Joyce gazed at her phone. "I've already gotten eight emails back, and they are furious. There are only fifteen trucks on the street. I'm sure we'll have quite a turnout for the protest."

"Then we'd better get moving on the supplies."

"I can take care of it, unless you want to join me?"

"I'd love to," Brenda said.

"Are you sure? I know it's a day off."

"Charlie has a ton of work to do, and I don't have to be anywhere until Sophie is done with school. Let me just say goodbye to Charlie and grab my purse and keys. We can take my car."

"Sounds good to me." Joyce slipped her purse over her shoulder and waited for Brenda near the door.

As Brenda drove towards the shopping district, Joyce reviewed her list on the phone.

"Let's see, we'll need the hardware store, and the craft store."

"Good, they're on the same road. We can park here and walk." Brenda parked across from a line of shops. She fed a few quarters into the meter then pointed to the end of the street. "The hardware store is down there, but the craft store is only a few doors down, so we can hit there first."

"Okay, we need some markers, poster boards, and maybe a bullhorn if they happen to have one."

"Hmm, maybe." As they began to cross the street towards the shops, Brenda stopped short. "Look, it's Vince." She grabbed Joyce by the elbow and pulled her back behind a van parked along the side of the road.

"Where?" Joyce peeked around the side of the van.

"There, near the butcher's shop." Brenda

pointed to a small shop a few buildings down from where they were hiding. "I think he's just going in."

"Yes, he is. We should follow him."

"And do what? Ask him if he's a killer?" Brenda edged back behind the van again. "I'm not sure that I want to risk surprising a man who might have killed and is likely at least armed."

"We'll just happen to be shopping for meat as well. No big deal, right?" Joyce shrugged.

"All right, let's do it." Brenda followed after Joyce, who was already halfway to the butcher shop.

"Oh, what a lovely shop!" Joyce exclaimed as she stepped through the door. Her gleeful voice drew the attention of everyone else in the store. The shop itself was rather small, with a counter that ran the length of the back. It had old world charm, as if it belonged in some quaint village somewhere. A woman and a man stood behind the counter while another customer placed his order. Vince was just about to walk through a door to the rear section of the shop. He paused, then turned to face both women as the door closed behind them.

"Joyce, Brenda. What are you doing here?" He offered a half-smile. "Not following me, are you?"

"We're here to buy some meat." Joyce raised an eyebrow. "Why are you here?"

"To do the same, of course. Great minds think alike, I suppose." Vince smirked.

"I suppose." Joyce narrowed her eyes. "Have you already placed your order?"

"I have a deal with the owner."

"Oh, I see." Joyce smiled. "That's nice."

"It is. If you order a large quantity, he gives you a discount. I don't imagine that you will need meat for your truck. Unless you're getting very creative with donuts." Vince smiled.

"No, we're just here to buy some meat for at home." Brenda cleared her throat.

"Ah, I see."

"And what are you going to do with a large quantity of meat?" Joyce met his eyes.

"Well, that's my secret, isn't it?" He grinned. "Maybe I've decided to go into a new business venture."

"Maybe?" She searched his expression.

"Well, Adam and I had a deal. He was going to sell me part ownership of his truck in exchange for money to buy the meat and other supplies so he could add hamburgers to his menu. Now that he's gone though, I guess I'll get in touch with his aunt and make a bid to take over his entire truck."

"You don't seem too heartbroken about that."

"Life gives you lemons, you buy a food truck." He shrugged. "It's not like Adam's going to be using it."

"Awful." Brenda frowned. "That's no way to talk about someone you considered a friend."

"I don't have friends, Brenda. I have business partners. I don't need the approval of anyone. Adam and I saw an opportunity to corner the market, so we went for it. Then he up and got himself killed. I wish he hadn't, but he did. I already paid for the meat, and it's not like I can return it. So, I've got to find a way to cover my losses. No need to be so sensitive."

"Forgive us if we're still grieving the death of our friend." Joyce frowned. "He was a fine young man."

"Sure, he was. But he's not here anymore. I'm not a religious person. Death is death to me. It's just a part of life. One day I'll be gone, too, and I can promise you there isn't going to be a soul around to shed a tear for me." He pushed through the door, ending their conversation. Joyce stepped closer to Brenda.

"Did you get all of that?"

"Yes, I did. I think Vince just hand-delivered us his motive for killing Adam."

"He wanted the truck for himself?" Brenda frowned. "But why would a man like him, a possible criminal, want to own a food truck?"

"Think about it. It would be the perfect setup for dealing drugs. It's mobile, it's a good cover if the cops come sniffing around." Joyce narrowed her eyes. "He's clever. I'll give him that. That must have been what that conversation I overheard was about."

"Then it would benefit him to kill Adam and take over the truck?" Brenda asked as they continued on to the craft supply store.

"Maybe, but Adam was great cover for him. Now, Vince will be under suspicion just because of who he is. But it's possible that if Vince mentioned the drug dealing to Adam that Adam was against it and wanted to back out of the deal, or Adam threatened to expose him."

"So he decided to kill him?" Brenda narrowed her eyes.

"Maybe, but drug dealing seems like a risky move for him to make if he really was planning on investing in Adam and the hot dog truck."

"That's true. It's still something to consider." Brenda nodded.

They spent the remainder of the afternoon purchasing supplies and creating signs for the protesters to carry. By the time Joyce left for the night, Brenda was exhausted. She put Sophie to bed and joined Charlie in the living room.

"Hey." Charlie pulled her close and kissed the side of her neck. "How did everything go?"

"Good, I guess." She filled him in on the details.

"That's interesting."

"It's all just so frustrating." She shook her head.

"I know it is, sweetheart. But this too shall pass. Just have patience." He patted her hand.

"Patience seems like the wrong thing to have. Shouldn't I be out there trying to solve the problem?" Brenda asked.

"Sometimes problems are too big for one person to solve. Then you just have to let go and let things fall into place."

"Maybe." She kissed the tip of his nose. "Any interest in helping me to forget about those problems?"

"Tons of interest." He grinned.

CHAPTER 10

*J*oyce and Brenda arrived at the truck early the next morning. As the owners of the trucks began to show up, Joyce reminded them about their planned protest and where they could pick up their signs. Brenda tried to get the oven to heat up correctly.

"Ugh, this thing is on the fritz again." She frowned, then gave it a forceful kick. "Maybe that will help."

"I'm sorry, Brenda, I guess we're going to have to get a new one." Joyce sighed as she stared at the oven. It seemed to her that money was starting to drain right out of the business. "Is it warming up at all?"

"Some, it's just that the temperature never seems

right. I've been using my own thermometer to gauge it. That will get us through for now."

"That's good at least." Joyce glanced through the window of the truck. "The other owners are all ready to join the protest this afternoon. Even Pete."

"Great." Brenda smiled. "Poor Pierce has no idea what's coming."

Right at the lunch hour, they all gathered at the entrance of Green Street with their signs and formed a line that blocked the road.

"This is it." Joyce shot a smile in Brenda's direction. "Time to find out if we can make a difference."

"I know we can!" Brenda held her sign up high, as did the other protesters. As fast as customers arrived, they were turned away. Soon a few news crews showed up to cover the protest. Not long after, Pierce's spotless car pulled up beside the crowd and parked. When he stepped out, a bolt of fear rushed through Joyce. She looked over at Brenda, whose eyes widened. Both women braced themselves for what might happen next.

"What is all of this about?" Pierce straightened his suit jacket and scowled across the gathered truck owners. "You wanted my attention, well, I'm here now. So what is the problem? Have I not supported you enough? Have I not made sure that you had everything that you needed out here?"

"Sure you have, Councilman." Joyce stepped forward from the line despite her racing heart and raised her voice even louder. "But what you failed to tell us was that you are attempting to rezone this street. Which means we will no longer be able to have our food trucks here."

"That's nonsense." He took a step towards her. "Who are you to tell me what I'm doing? You've barely been here a month and yet you think you're calling the shots?" His gaze shifted to the other truck owners in the crowd. "She's just trying to stir things up. Can't you see that?"

"Then what is this article all about?" Joyce reached into her pocket and pulled out the article. When she thrust it towards him, he snatched it out of her hands. He was silent as he read over it, then looked up at her with a furrowed brow.

"You should really learn a little bit about politics before you start creating so much drama. Yes, I said this, but that doesn't mean I'm going to do it. Sometimes you have to say things to smooth the feathers of one group of people. It doesn't mean that I'm going to go through with it and continue to push for the rezoning. That would be absurd. What would I gain from moving you all out of here, or even shutting some of you down? Nothing!"

"I know there's something." Joyce glared at him. "I just haven't figured out what it is yet."

"Because there is nothing, because you decided to cause a problem when there was no need for one. Hey!" He looked back at the others blocking the street. "How many of you are losing customers right now because you listened to what one uninformed woman had to say? Get back to your trucks. Maybe you can still make some money today. You're wasting your time here." He glared in Joyce's direction. "Not all of them have an inheritance to fall back on, you know. They need to make a living."

"I know I'm not wrong. Why would you say that you support the rezoning if you don't? I know you're up to something." She stared hard into his eyes.

"Well, let's just see how far all of this knowing gets you. Shall we?" He shook his head and turned back to his car. The sound of signs clattering to the ground filled the air as the other protesters returned to their trucks. Soon, only Brenda still held a sign.

"I'm so sorry, Brenda. I am so embarrassed, and I pulled you into all of it. I can't believe that I've put us in this position. If the other truck owners hate us, we are going to have nothing but problems. It'll be the end." She frowned.

"It's all right, Joyce, don't worry. We're going to get all of this straightened out." Brenda looked into her eyes.

"How? Now everyone thinks we got it wrong and whipped them into some kind of frenzy that could have cost them all a lot."

"But that's not what happened. You and I both know the truth. Pierce can tell all the lies he wants, but soon enough the truth will come out, and everyone will know who the liar is."

"I hope so. But what if it doesn't? What if Adam's death remains unsolved, and Green Street gets rezoned, and…"

"Why don't we just keep the truck closed and go have a late lunch?" Brenda patted her shoulder. "We don't get enough opportunity to just relax and enjoy each other's company. We've let all of this stress weigh too heavily on us. We need a break."

"I agree, but is this really the best time for that?"

"Why not? We're not going to have many more customers today. Charlie isn't expecting me home until later this afternoon. Let's just go have a relaxing lunch. I've heard the diner on the corner is really great."

"Okay, I guess it wouldn't hurt to have a good meal. Cooking for one doesn't always inspire a wide range of cuisine."

"Great. I'll clean up, you close up the register, and we'll be out of here in no time."

"I guess that's better than facing a bunch of angry truck owners." Joyce headed back towards the truck while Brenda collected all of the signs that had been left behind.

A few minutes later, Brenda joined Joyce in the truck to make sure all of the supplies were put away and the counters were tidy.

As Joyce finished up the register paperwork, she noticed someone walk past the truck. A moment later, she saw that it was Pete. He and another truck owner, Ricco, paused not far from her truck and began to talk.

She looked out at them as their discussion continued. Right away, she picked up that Pete was upset. Joyce put her finger to her lips and used the other hand to gesture for Brenda to come over and listen.

"She's crazy, Pete. She was wrong, you heard what Pierce said."

Brenda glanced over at Joyce with a raised eyebrow.

"No, she's not crazy. She's right. Pierce is trying to shut this whole place down. I'm not going to let that happen."

"Well, I'm not going to upset Pierce just because some old lady has a hunch." Ricco shook his head and crossed his arms.

Joyce clucked her tongue and whispered, "Rude."

Brenda leaned closer to the window and stared at the two men. They were so engrossed in their conversation that they didn't notice Joyce or Brenda.

"You do what you want, but I'm telling you right now, Joyce knows what she's talking about. I've suspected Pierce for a while. I'm going to make sure everyone around here finds out the truth."

As Pete walked away from Ricco, Joyce took a deep breath and leaned back from the window. "It looks like at least Pete is on our side."

"See? I told you everything would be fine."

"I'm not sure how that makes it fine."

"Pete has been here a long time. I'm sure that he'll be a voice of reason when it comes to the other truck owners."

"Maybe." Joyce frowned as she watched Pete walk back towards his truck. "But there's something about that man that worries me. I mean Pete could be the murderer. He might just be against the rezoning of Green Street because he is way too protective of his business."

"I understand, and I still think it might be him. However, it's nice to know we have an ally. I'm done here, are you ready to go?"

"Sure, I just need my purse." Once Joyce had it, they left the truck. She paused to lock the door. A flash of light from the sun bounced off the key. Her chest tightened. They still had no idea who killed Adam. Every time she thought of that, her heart dropped.

"I'll meet you over there." Brenda waved to her as she approached her car. Joyce lingered for a moment beside hers. She looked back at the row of trucks. How much longer would she be able to call Green Street her home away from home? Maybe the other truck owners were upset with her at the moment, but in many ways, some of them had become like a second family to her. She knew she was right about Pierce. The problem was she needed to prove it, and she couldn't figure out why he would want to shut down Green Street to the food trucks.

CHAPTER 11

When Joyce pulled into the parking lot of the diner, she was startled to see Pierce's fancy car. She stared at it for a moment, then stepped out of the car. Brenda was a few spots away and walked towards her. Both froze as they saw Pierce step out of the diner.

"Don't let him see us. After today, I don't think he's going to be too friendly." Brenda stood close to Joyce. Luckily, Pierce walked quickly to his car and climbed in. A moment later, he tore out of the parking lot.

"He seems upset." Joyce raised an eyebrow. "I guess we touched a nerve."

As they walked into the diner, they were greeted by a faint smile from a waitress as a menu was thrust into their hands. The waitress led them to a small table, then walked away without taking their drink order.

"What do you think all of that is about?" Brenda frowned. "She's not very friendly."

"I'm not sure. Maybe she's just having an off day, or maybe news of my folly has preceded us."

"Maybe." Brenda glanced over the menu. Joyce did as well, but couldn't get her eyes to focus on it.

"You know if Pierce is willing to lie like that, then I think he is more than capable of killing Adam."

"Wow." Brenda lowered the menu and looked across the table at Joyce. "That is a big leap."

"Is it though?" She pursed her lips. "If we know that Pierce is trying to shut down Green Street, maybe Adam found that out, too. Maybe he had some kind of evidence to prove it and was going to bring attention to it."

"That's an interesting thought." Brenda closed her eyes for a moment. "Yes, I can see how that could work. Pierce didn't want too much attention on his plans, and maybe Adam was furious about the shut down, so he was going to expose Pierce, and possibly even Cooper about taking bribes as well."

"Which would get Pierce into even more trouble, as he's the one who brought Cooper's company in to run most of the local council events."

"Are you two ready to order?" The waitress paused beside their table. She looked between them with some disdain in her expression.

"Have we done something to offend you?" Joyce settled her gaze on the young woman. "Because I have to say, I'm accustomed to a little better service than this."

"No, you haven't done anything wrong. I just know who you are. You run one of the trucks on the street, right?" She shook her head. "You guys steal all of our customers. I get bare bones tips because of you."

"Because of us?" Brenda laughed. "I think it might be more because of your attitude."

"No, it's true. Everyone goes to the trucks because it's quick and cheap. No one wants to come into the diner." She frowned. "I don't mean to give you the cold shoulder, but I'm just so frustrated by it."

"I see." Brenda nodded. "I can understand how that would be frustrating."

"Just do us a favor and go easy on us. We've had a rough morning. Besides, unless your main sales are donuts, we're not your competition," Joyce said.

"Oh. Are you the ones with the donut truck?" Her eyes widened. "I had one of those baked donuts the other day, they are so good!"

"Thank you." Brenda smiled. "Maybe next time we come in, we'll bring some for the staff here."

"Sure, that would be great. Now, what can I get for you?"

After they gave their orders, the waitress walked away. Joyce lowered her voice. "Wow, that was not a friendly welcome."

"Should we add her to the list of suspects?" Brenda did her best to hide a smile.

"I think we can rule her out. Now, what are we going to do about Pierce?"

"We could go to Detective Crackle and tell him what we suspect." Brenda rested her hands on the table and took a deep breath.

"But Brenda, it's not that simple. We can tell Detective Crackle what we think might have happened, but without any proof, he's not going to be able to do anything about it. You don't just arrest someone, and especially a man like Pierce, on a whim. You have to have solid proof that is going to stand up in court." Joyce turned to look out through the front window of the diner. "I bet you that all of the people that work around us don't believe that they're about to have everything ripped out from under them. Maybe Adam died because he knew too much. Pierce can't get away with this. We can't let that happen."

"So what do you suggest? You know I agree with you, but we have to have some kind of plan."

"My suggestion is that we get that proof ourselves." Joyce cleared her throat and tilted her head to the side. "Or I do."

"No, none of that. If we're going to do this, we're both in on it." Brenda fell silent as the waitress arrived with their burgers. Once they were delivered, she locked her eyes on Joyce. "We're in this together, Joyce. You're not doing anything reckless or stupid unless we're doing it together."

"That's very sweet of you. I'll tell you what. I will go to Detective Crackle with what we have. And if he can do something about it, then we'll wait it out. But if he can't, then we'll figure out a way to try to get the proof ourselves."

"That I can live with." Brenda nodded.

"I still can't get the fact that Adam was going to add burgers to his menu out of my mind though," Joyce said as she stared at her hamburger.

"You still think that might have something to do with Adam's murder."

"I think it is a possibility. Pete might be on our side about Green Street because he is obsessed with protecting his business."

"You think that maybe he is so obsessed that he killed Adam to protect his own business?" Brenda's eyes widened.

"Yes, exactly."

"Okay, so we have three prime suspects."

"Well, four really, don't forget Vince."

"Okay, Pete, Pierce, Cooper, and Vince. It doesn't really narrow it down much, does it?"

"No, it doesn't. But four it is. And I'll tell Detective Crackle about all of them." Joyce nodded.

After their meal, Brenda drove home. She was still a little wound up from the failed protest and wondered if Charlie would be upset that he'd sent reporters to witness the debacle. She stopped by to pick up Sophie from school and decided to take her for an ice cream as a treat. Before they left for the ice cream shop, she texted Charlie to let him know she had Sophie and what they planned to do. He responded swiftly.

Sounds good. Bring me some Rocky Road.

Brenda smiled at his request. It was one of his

favorite flavors of ice cream, but it also meant he'd hit a block on one of his stories. He always used ice cream to try to get out of a rut. She ordered for all of them, then drove home so that they could eat it together. While Sophie managed to get ice cream on both her cheeks and chin, Brenda explained what happened at the protest.

"Well, Pierce is a bald-faced liar, that's for sure. You're right for thinking he's up to something. I looked into his financial records, the ones that I could access, and they are outrageous. I don't think there's any way that he doesn't have some kind of illegal funding flowing in. His house alone is worth far more than his salary could ever support."

"Interesting. But no clues as to where the money might be coming from?"

"Not just yet." He frowned. "I would suspect though that he gets some kickbacks from those who are accepting bribes from the truck owners and maybe even the truck owners themselves. I imagine that isn't the only pot he's got his hand in."

"He could be doing it all over. Not just on Green Street." She sighed. "Maybe he's just too big to take down."

"No way, sweetie. The bigger they are, the

harder they fall. You just have to find the crack and smash it."

"What if there isn't one?" Brenda asked with frustration.

"Oh, trust me, all of the big players have one."

"That doesn't mean they are murderers."

"True." Charlie nodded. "I also looked into some of the truck owners and employees. The only one that raised a red flag was Pete."

"Really?"

"Yes, there is nothing recent, but he has a long list of arrests, many for violent crimes."

"That's interesting."

"What's more interesting is that one of those arrests, the most recent one, was for assaulting one of the food truck owners that is now no longer on Green Street. They had a fight. I can't see what it was over, but it got pretty messy."

"Wow. It certainly moves him up the suspect list. Joyce and I were discussing him before. If he was violent and overprotective of his business, that could be a lethal combination."

"It could be. I will keep looking."

"You're so good to me, Charlie."

"Just keep that in mind, always." He caught her

hand and brought the back of it to his lips. "Anything for you."

Her heart warmed in reaction to his words, but the heavy weight of uncertainty still kept the smile from her lips.

"I love you, too, Charlie."

"Great, then you'll forgive me, because I do need to get some work done."

"Go on." She pointed to his office. "One of us has to be successful."

"Don't give up hope." Charlie disappeared into his office.

Brenda decided to spend some time thinking of new recipes for the donut truck. It always relaxed her to think about baking, and she needed a break from trying to work out who the murderer was.

~

A couple of hours later, just as Brenda started to prepare dinner, Charlie stepped back out of his office. She glanced over at him, and the lack of color in his face told her that something terrible had happened.

"Charlie, what is it?"

"I just heard from a colleague. There's been another murder."

"What? What do you mean?" Brenda dropped the spoon she held onto the floor. "Not Joyce?"

"No, not Joyce." He stepped closer to her and lowered his voice. "Pete."

"Pete?" She stared at him with disbelief.

"He was found dead near the dumpster, and it's clearly a murder. He was shot."

"Oh no, that's awful! I just don't understand this." Brenda shook her head.

"I don't either." He pulled her close and wrapped his arms around her. "I'm not so sure you should go back to work until all of this settles down."

"Let me talk to Joyce about it. All right?" She leaned back and looked into his eyes.

"Yes, all right." He frowned. "I'll finish up dinner. Use my office so Sophie won't interrupt you."

"Thanks." She stepped into the office then closed the door behind her. She selected Joyce's name from her list of contacts. A second later, her friend picked up the phone.

"No, I haven't managed to see Detective Crackle

yet." Joyce spoke up before Brenda could say a word.

"Joyce, you're not going to believe this."

"What is it, Brenda? You sound upset. What's going on?"

"They just found Pete. Dead!"

"Pete?" Joyce gasped. "How?"

"Shot, near the dumpster. I only know because one of Charlie's co-workers called him to let him know. He was found sometime this evening. That's all I know."

"Oh, this is horrible. Poor Pete. This is crazy. Who is doing this?"

"Do you think the deaths are related?" Brenda asked.

"How can they not be? So close together. That can't be a coincidence."

"Maybe someone is out to get food truck owners? I don't know, but Charlie is upset. He doesn't want me to go back to work on the truck. I mean, I will of course, but…"

"I understand. I need to talk to Detective Crackle first thing tomorrow. Maybe he will be willing to put a patrol car on Green Street. I understand why Charlie is worried. Let's just take it one step at a time. Hopefully this will be solved quickly."

"All right, Joyce. Sorry to spring this on you, but I thought you'd want to know as soon as I did."

"I do. Thanks." Joyce grew silent for a moment, then spoke up again. "Pete was our only supporter after the protest. It may mean nothing, but it may mean everything, too. We do need to be careful."

"I will be."

"In the morning, I will speak to Detective Crackle."

"Good, let me know if you need anything." Brenda hung up the phone and stared into empty space for a moment. If Pete was dead, who might be next?

~

First thing in the morning, Joyce drove straight to the police station. She requested a meeting with Detective Crackle and was not deterred by the desk sergeant claiming he was not available.

"Please tell him it's Joyce from the donut truck and that I want to speak with him."

"All right, I'll give it a shot." One phone call later, she was escorted to a private room. As she sat alone, she tried to gather her thoughts, but she couldn't get a clear read on who did this.

When the door swung open, she looked up to find Detective Crackle standing just outside the room.

"Joyce, I guess you heard?" He sat down across from her.

"Yes, I heard. Have you questioned Pierce about the murder yet?"

"Councilman Pierce?" He raised an eyebrow. "No."

"Well, you should. Pete was the only one who supported our protest. And Melvin Cooper is taking bribes, and Pierce is trying to shut down Green Street, and…"

"Okay, take a breath, Joyce." Detective Crackle leaned forward across the table. "We'll get to all of that, I promise. Wherever there is credible evidence, the investigation is going to head in that direction."

"So? Who is your main suspect?"

"I can't tell you that."

"Do you even have one?" She frowned. "I thought maybe it was Vince."

"Really? Why?" He looked at her intently.

"He has a criminal history. He was trying to go into business with Adam. Maybe he wanted the whole business for himself. Or maybe he wanted to use it as a front for drug dealing."

"I can see you have thought this through." He leaned back in his chair. "We are investigating all avenues."

"Thank you, Detective Crackle. We really want this solved so we can go back to work."

"I understand. I'm investigating the situation. Right now I haven't even been able to establish a connection between the two crimes. Now I know that it may be easy to assume that they are related, but really they are more different than they are similar. Adam was struck and killed, and Pete was shot. There's a big difference between those types of murders. At this time, we still don't have a solid motive for Adam's murder, while Pete had quite a few enemies that we are sorting through right now."

"Is there anything I can do to help? Anything that would speed this investigation along?"

"What I need from you is patience." He met her eyes. "I need you to let me do my job so that we can find some answers."

"I understand that, but we can't wait much longer for answers. Not only are we afraid that we may be in danger, but if we keep losing revenue, I'm going to have to shut down the truck. I hope that you can see why I'm concerned."

"Yes, I can. You're not the only one that is concerned either. I've had lots of calls about these two murders. However, taking phone calls and these kinds of meetings pulls me away from the work that I need to do in order to crack the case. As long as I'm distracted, the criminal has extra time to get away. So, if you don't mind?" He gestured towards the door.

"I don't. I'm sorry for taking up your time." She stood up and offered her hand across the desk.

"Joyce." He took her hand in a firm shake, then stood up as well. "I would rather you let me handle the investigation."

"Of course." She nodded, but she still had no intention of not investigating the murder. "And by the way, I think that the murder weapon in Adam's case was the lid of a hot dog bin."

"I know that." He narrowed his eyes. "How did you know that?"

"I have my ways." She smiled.

He nodded as she stepped past him and out the door. Although the meeting hadn't been as productive as Joyce had hoped, she was relieved to know that Detective Crackle was actively working on the case. She felt a sense of confidence in the detective's ability to solve the murders, but there was still no harm in her helping him. After she left the police station, she placed a call to Brenda.

"How did it go?"

"It went okay. I told him who we thought might be the culprits. Hopefully he'll look into it, but we can't wait that long. I think that we need to look more closely at Pierce. I don't know if the police will look at him closely enough because of his influence. We need to make a plan," Joyce said. "Let's meet at my place and we can figure things out."

"Okay, I can be there in a half hour," Brenda said enthusiastically.

"Perfect."

Joyce hung up the phone, then drove back towards her house. Her heart raced in time with the panicked thoughts that flooded her mind. But one particular thought silenced the rest. She could not let someone get away with murder.

CHAPTER 12

*W*hen Joyce arrived at home, she checked to see if Pierce was in his office. One call to his secretary revealed that he was. She thought about setting up a meeting, but after their encounter, she guessed that he would have very little interest in that. A surprise attack was a better idea. When there was a knock at the door, she realized that Brenda had arrived.

"Come on in!" She stood up just as Brenda stepped inside.

"All right, what's the plan? Break in and ransack the place?"

"Ha, nothing like that. Pierce is in his office, so I say we go down there. He might be willing to let us into his office to talk to him."

"And if he does?" Brenda frowned.

"If he does, then we'll have a chance to look around. In fact, what would be even better is if one of us is able to distract him so the other can be alone in the office."

"How could we do that?"

"Well, we haven't returned his suit jacket yet. I think that could be our way in," Joyce suggested.

"Oh, good idea, that's perfect. Do you still have it?" Brenda asked.

"Yes, I've been meaning to give it back but with everything that's happened, I just didn't get around to it."

"Still, finding a way to distract him might be difficult."

"You're right, but it's worth a try, and if we're going to do this, we need to do it now. He might be leaving the office soon. Let me just grab the jacket."

On the drive to Pierce's office, Joyce came up with a plan to distract him.

"We'll ask for coffee, and then one of us will spill that coffee on Pierce's jacket. Then offer to clean it for him if he changes out of it, and offer him his freshly cleaned suit jacket. Hopefully, he'll be polite enough to excuse himself to change. Just make sure you get some on his shirt, too. I'm sure he has a spare in his office that he'll want to change into."

"Me?" Brenda's eyes widened. "I have to do the spilling?"

"Well, you do have a history of ruining suit jackets." Joyce grinned.

"Very funny." Brenda frowned. "What if he doesn't change? Or they won't give us coffee?"

"Then I guess we'll just have to think of something else. But we're here now, so let's give it a shot." Joyce grabbed the jacket and stepped out of the car. When they entered the office, the secretary looked up with surprise.

"There are no more appointments today."

"Oh, this isn't exactly an appointment, it's more like an apology actually. I have the councilman's jacket to return to him, and my business partner and I wanted to discuss the protest."

"Oh, you two were responsible for that?" She clucked her tongue. "Let me see if he has time to speak with you." She picked up the phone on her desk and spoke quietly for a few minutes. Then the door to her right swung open, and Pierce filled it.

"Ladies." His jaw was set.

"Mr. Pierce, I know after yesterday that you probably don't want to give us a minute of your time, but we would both really appreciate it if we could have a quick chat."

"Is that my jacket?" He locked his eyes on the jacket she held.

"Yes, it is." Joyce held it out. "I think you'll find that it is perfectly cleaned."

"Hm." He lifted the plastic to look it over, then tilted his head towards the door of his office. "Come in."

Joyce started towards the door, then paused and looked back at the secretary. "Is there any coffee? I don't care if it's old, Brenda and I will both take a cup, please. If you don't mind?" She smiled inwardly at the fact that it was much easier to get away with being demanding now that she was a bit older.

"Uh, sure, I guess." The secretary stood up and headed down the hall. Joyce studied the office as she stepped inside. It was spotless, with everything neat and tidy. However, there was a stack of folders and papers in a tray on one side of the desk. She was sure if she could find something to prove that the councilman really was pushing to have the street rezoned, she could at least get the owners of the trucks behind her again.

"Please, sit." Pierce pointed to two chairs in

front of his desk. "My secretary said you are here to apologize?"

"Yes." Joyce cleared her throat. "We should never have caused such chaos."

"No, you shouldn't have." He straightened his tie and stared at them both. "I'm sure you're aware that I could revoke your permit to sell on Green Street. Perhaps if I was the dishonest person that you seem to think I am, I would do that. But since I'm not, and you're here to apologize, I will let this slide."

"Thank you so much, sir. I can get a little over-eager about things. Brenda here, she tries to calm me down, but you know, I just get carried away."

"You should listen to Brenda." He locked eyes with her. "She seems to be the level-headed one."

"Coffee." The secretary brought them each a mug of coffee. Brenda was relieved when she felt that it wasn't very hot.

"Thank you." Pierce nodded. "You can go on your break."

"Thank you, sir."

"As I was saying, Joyce, next time, follow Brenda's advice."

"I do like to give people the benefit of the doubt, Mr. Pierce. But I still don't understand why you would be involved in the fight to rezone the street at all, even if it is just for show and to keep people happy as you say." Joyce locked her eyes to his.

"And that's not for you to understand. I am in the position I am for a reason, and it's not because I'm stupid. You'll just have to trust that I'm working for everyone's best interests. Now, if that's all." He stood up and held out his hand to Brenda. Brenda gritted her teeth. She knew it was now or never. Could she really fling a cup of coffee on the councilman? She stood up and took a step forward to reach the councilman's hand. As she did, she felt her foot catch on something. It only took a second for her to realize that Joyce had tripped her. The coffee flung forward out of her cup as she grabbed onto the desk to steady herself. It splashed all over Pierce's jacket and the white button-up shirt underneath.

"Oh no!" he gasped.

"I'm so sorry!" Brenda gulped.

Joyce jumped up. "Oh, Mr. Pierce, you need to get that coffee stain out right now! Good thing you have another jacket to wear."

"Good thing?" he shouted. "This is the second time!"

"And we'll have everything cleaned again. I'm so sorry. I just don't know what's wrong with her.

Brenda, are you all right? Maybe you need to see a doctor about that clumsiness."

"Yes, maybe." Brenda sighed. "Please Mr. Pierce, if you give me your shirt, I can soak it for you. Do you have another shirt you can change into?"

"Yes, of course." He huffed and opened a door to a small closet. After he snatched a shirt from it, he grabbed his freshly cleaned suit jacket and stalked out of the office. Brenda followed after him.

"I'll clean up the mess in here." Joyce called after them. She hurried down the same hall that the secretary had and grabbed some paper towels. As quickly as she could, she mopped up the few drips of coffee that landed on the desk. Then she began to go through the stack of files on top of it.

As she sorted through the papers, she soon found that while Pierce had a lot of paperwork, none of it had anything to do with the street being rezoned. She glanced at her watch and noticed that five minutes had already slid by. Pierce wouldn't be gone for long, and she really didn't want to be caught. In desperation, she snapped a few pictures of different things in the office. Maybe when she had time to look at them closely, she would find something.

On a whim, she decided to take pictures of his personal photographs that hung on the wall behind his desk. With the tissue in her hand, she tried to open the desk drawer directly in front of Pierce's chair. After one tug, she found it was locked up tight. If she had more time she might have been able to find a way to unlock it, but the sound of footsteps in the hallway told her that her time was up. She glanced around quickly to make sure that everything was back in place then managed to drop back into her chair just before the door swung open. Brenda followed Pierce into the room and went to stand next to Joyce. Pierce turned towards them.

"Ladies, I think that you've taken up enough of my time." He tilted his head towards the door. "Please, do me a favor, and get your facts straight before you ever even think about stirring up this kind of trouble again."

"We will, Mr. Pierce. Thank you for your time," Joyce said.

"Sorry again." Brenda cringed.

"Just, maybe keep your distance around me, hmm?" Pierce shook his head. Brenda and Joyce hurried back out to the car.

"Did you find anything?" Brenda smiled eagerly as she pulled away from the building.

"No, I didn't. I'm sorry, Brenda. I really thought that would work, but I guess I was wrong." She stared out through the side window.

"Hey, Joyce, don't be upset. You did what you could. Maybe the police will have better luck."

"I doubt that Detective Crackle is even going to look into Pierce." She slapped her knee with exasperation. "I bet you that as far as the police know, he is an upstanding citizen. Maybe if I knew how to pick locks." She sighed and closed her eyes.

"Don't be so hard on yourself, Joyce. We're going to figure this out."

"I did take some pictures. Maybe there will be something to see there, but I doubt it."

"Oh? What kind of pictures?"

"Just of different areas of the office. I didn't really have time to look through everything, so I thought there might possibly be something that I overlooked."

"Can you send them to me?"

"Sure, I'll do that right now." Joyce scrolled through her phone and sent the pictures off to Brenda. "Let's look them over tonight. Maybe we'll find something. I know you have to get home, but let me know if you notice anything unusual or interesting."

"I will." She pulled into Joyce's driveway and parked beside her car. "Joyce, try to remember, you're not the detective here. We can try to help, but you shouldn't beat yourself up if we don't get anywhere."

"I'll try." She smiled. "Thanks."

CHAPTER 13

*B*efore Joyce's eyes even opened in the morning, her cell phone rang. She fumbled for it and saw that it was Brenda.

"Hello?"

"Can we meet for breakfast? At the diner?"

"Mmhm, I'll be there." She stifled a yawn. "Give me twenty minutes."

"Take forty, I have to get Sophie to school first."

"Okay, I'll see you there." As Joyce got dressed, she wondered what Brenda might have found. Joyce hoped that she might run into Vince. Given his criminal history, she imagined he was the police's prime suspect. However, she wanted to find out what Brenda might have discovered first. When she arrived at the diner, Brenda was already there, seated at the same table they'd been at before.

"Morning, Brenda."

"Morning, Joyce. Sorry to call so early. I got a little excited. I realized something. The girlfriend. It's what we've been forgetting to look into. I remember in those pictures that you sent me of the inside of Adam's truck, there was a tiny wallet photograph of a woman pinned up on the wall. Remember, you found it behind the other photos? I bet that's her." She skimmed through the photographs on her phone, then paused on the one with the small picture. "It's too small to see her face, but I can get Charlie to enhance it. Hold on, I'll send it to him right now." She texted the picture and request to Charlie, then looked across the table at Joyce. "This might be the break that we need."

"That would be good, because I am still struggling to tie all of this together. First, we have Pierce, who clearly has some kind of motive to shut down the trucks on Green Street. But for the life of me, I can't figure out what the motive is and why he would want to kill Adam. And what about Pete? I mean there are easier ways to force a shutdown than through murder. Pierce has so much to lose, I can't imagine him getting involved in all of this."

"Maybe, but he's also a man with power, and as Charlie told me, a man with power doesn't like to be questioned. Maybe Adam asked one too many questions, and Pierce needed him to be quiet?"

"Maybe." Joyce frowned and gazed down at the food on her plate. "I just wish there was a way to get some evidence of why Pierce would want to shut down Green Street. I got nothing but pictures from his office."

"Let's look at those again, shall we?" Brenda pulled them up on her phone and began to slowly look through them. "Notice the photographs on the table behind his desk?"

"Yes?" Joyce looked at the same photographs on her phone.

"One of them is of this very diner. With a few people standing in front. Can you tell who it is?"

"It looks like Pierce, and two other people. I'm not sure who. Maybe his wife? And Melvin?"

"Yes, maybe. That's odd, don't you think?"

"Why?" Joyce glanced up at her. "We know he likes this place. He was leaving here the last time we came."

"Yes, he was. But I like a lot of restaurants. I don't take family pictures in front of them, and even if I did, I wouldn't choose that picture as one to display in my office. Right?"

"I guess not." Joyce pursed her lips as she studied the photograph. "So why did he?"

"It might be a coincidence, but maybe it's important to him. Maybe we should look into this diner."

"Maybe." Joyce raised her hand to summon the waitress. Brenda smiled as she walked over.

"Is everything okay here?"

"Can you tell me who owns this restaurant?" Joyce locked eyes with her.

"Leighann Chambers." She shrugged. "She's the only owner as far as I know."

"Thank you very much for your help." Joyce finished the last bite of her food. "Let's go, Brenda. I think we might have a lead."

As they left the table, Joyce looked back at the waitress, who hurried over to the manager. She looked flushed as she spoke to the woman in charge. Joyce paused long enough to lip read snippets of their conversation.

"They wanted to know who owned the restaurant."

"I knew this would come out eventually."

"Joyce?" Brenda held the door open for her. "Are you all right?"

"Yes, yes I am, and we are definitely on to something. I hope Charlie doesn't mind a little company."

~

When Brenda and Joyce arrived at Brenda's house, Charlie and Sophie were playing a game of cards at the dining room table.

"Mommy!" Sophie jumped up and hugged her. Then she flung her arms around Joyce as well. "Hi Joyce!"

"Oh, that should be Mrs…" Charlie began.

"No please, Joyce is fine." She ruffled the little girl's hair. "You are such a good hugger, Sophie. Thank you so much."

"You're welcome." Sophie grinned. "I just beat Daddy three times in a row!"

"In a row?" Joyce laughed. "Sounds like he might need a break."

"I lost all of my crackers." Charlie sighed. "Sophie, let's go play outside and let Mommy and Joyce work."

"No, I'll take her outside. Joyce needs your help with something." Brenda grabbed Sophie's jacket and led her out through the back door.

"What do you need my help with?" Charlie looked up at her. "I already blew up the picture, if that's what it is, and you're not going to believe who it is."

"Not just that. I need to know everything there is to know about Leighann Chambers. Who was the picture of?" She followed him into his office.

"Kathy Pierce." He woke up the monitor and revealed the enlarged photograph.

"As in Councilman Pierce's wife?" Her eyes widened.

"The one and only. Well, so far. I'm guessing that may change in the future."

"So, you think she and Adam were having an affair?"

"I think it's hard not to make assumptions." He frowned. "From what Brenda told me about your meeting at the comic book shop, she fits the description. Very wealthy, the relationship would have to be kept secret, and if Pierce found out, well, there's your motivation for murder."

"Yes, there it is." She sank down into a chair beside him. "Wow."

"Yes, wow." He shook his head. "I'll never understand how people with such wealth can be so unhappy."

"Maybe she wasn't unhappy. Maybe she just likes younger men."

"Ouch. I guess that's possible." He nodded. "Now, as for Leighann Chambers." He did a quick search and pulled up a website. "Well, according to this, she is Pierce's youngest sister, or half-sister I should say."

"A half-sister? I didn't even know he had one. I didn't find any mention of her when I was doing research on him."

"I guess it's not something he advertises, as she was the product of an affair between his father and her mother, one of his employees."

"Wow. If Leighann owns the diner, and clearly Pierce still has a friendly relationship with her, then that might explain why he really wanted to shut down Green Street."

"Oh?" He raised an eyebrow.

"The first time we went to the diner, the waitress was complaining about how much business they lose to the food trucks. If the street was rezoned, then the only dining option would be Pierce's sister's diner. That would give her a big boost in customers."

"Yes, it would." He snapped his fingers. "But there's still one problem. There's no proof."

"And we still don't know why Pete was killed. Unless he was having an affair with the wife as well."

"Brenda mentioned that he was the only one who supported the protest against Pierce. He was killed not long after that. Maybe Pierce was upset that Pete was trying to tell the truth and bring attention to the fact that he supported the rezoning."

"It's possible. If Pierce had already killed once, maybe he didn't see a big issue with killing again."

"Maybe not." He sighed and ran his hand back through his brown curls. "It seems to me Pierce is the one with the motive. Adam was more than likely sleeping with his wife, and maybe he thought revealing the truth about Pierce would give him the opportunity to be with Kathy. I don't think I have to tell you this again, but this is such a dangerous situation. You're dealing with a powerful and well-liked politician who is used to getting what he wants. The moment you start to make accusations, you're going to be in danger. Without any proof, the police won't be able to offer you any protection."

"I know, I know. You're not going to want Brenda involved in this. And you're right. She shouldn't be." She stood up from her chair and adjusted her purse strap on her shoulder.

"Where are you going?" He studied her expression. "You look like you're up to something."

"I'm going to speak to Pierce's wife. If she was in a relationship with Adam, then she should be able to tell me something about his final days and whether her husband found out about their affair."

"That seems like a risky conversation to have with someone whose husband might be a murderer. How do you know that she wasn't involved? Maybe Adam threatened to expose their affair, and she killed him herself." He stood up from his chair. "You have to consider all of the possibilities."

"I know that, and I think that I am. But I have a better chance of finding out the truth if I talk to her directly than I do if I sniff around for a few weeks. I think it's worth the risk. I'll be subtle, and maybe I'll find out something."

"Then I'll come with you." He reached for his keys on the desk.

"No, you won't." Joyce patted his hand before he could pick up his keys. "You need to stay here and make sure that Brenda is safe and stays here. That's your job. Nothing else."

"You may feel that way, Joyce, but I don't. Now I may have never met your husband, but I suspect that if he was here, he would warn you that going alone is a very bad idea."

"He probably would. But he would also be the first one to go alone, into far more dangerous situations. Though I appreciate your concern, Charlie, this is something that is best done alone. Most women are not going to be willing to confess their affair with another man present." She smiled and gave him a light pat on the shoulder. "However, it is nice to know that you care. Please don't tell Brenda where I'm going. She'll want to tag along, and as you said, it's best if she doesn't. I will let you both know what happens after I speak with her, okay?"

"I guess I have no choice but to agree."

"I guess not." She smiled, winked at him, then turned and left the house. When she reached her car, she felt a slight shudder of fear. Was he right? Was she being foolish? She pushed past the concern and drove in the direction of Pierce's address. Although it was later in the day, she knew that Pierce would not be home. He had business meetings on his schedule all day, according to what Charlie looked up. Whether or not Kathy would be home was something she couldn't be sure of, but it was worth a shot.

When Joyce pulled into the driveway, she

noticed two cars. She guessed one belonged to Kathy due to its bright purple shade. The other was older, beat-up, and seemed quite out of place surrounded by the opulence of the three-story, two-winged mansion. Even her own car, which was a few years old, stuck out like a sore thumb. This was a place that only the rich visited. Even more intimidated than before, she considered turning around. However, the presence of the other car made her curious. Adam was not a wealthy man when he died. Perhaps Mrs. Pierce had an affinity for young working-class men. If that was the case, then she might have already moved on to a new beau.

After a few deep breaths, Joyce walked up to the front door and pressed the doorbell. It played classical music instead of any kind of ring. She wondered if anyone inside would even hear it. Just as she was about to knock, the door swung open.

"Oh, Mrs. Pierce, hello." Joyce smiled.

"I thought I was the one that should be surprised, as I was not expecting anyone, but my, you're as white as a ghost. Are you ill?"

"No." Joyce cleared her throat and took a good look at Kathy. She was adorned from head to toe in a gold-colored dress with a dramatic low-cut neckline and a sweeping skirt that drifted around her ankles. Paired with high heels and a diamond neck-lace, it was clear that she intended to go out that evening. "I'm sorry to interrupt you. It's just, I have something to discuss with you, and I think it will be important to you. It's about Adam Sonders."

"Who?" Her eyes widened. She reached up and touched the perfectly coiffed hair piled on the top of her head. "I'm sure it can't be that important to me."

"Joyce?" A familiar voice called out to her before the man that it belonged to stepped into the foyer.

"Detective Crackle." Joyce gritted her teeth.

"What are you doing here?" He squinted as he scrutinized her. "I wasn't aware that you and Mrs. Pierce knew each other."

"We don't." Kathy frowned. "At least I don't recall us ever meeting. Am I mistaken, Joyce?" She raised a dark, thin eyebrow.

"No, you're not mistaken. I'm sorry, this was a misunderstanding. I should go." She started to step back through the door.

"No, wait." Kathy grabbed her by the curve of her elbow. "You should stay. Detective Crackle was just leaving. Weren't you, Detective Crackle?" She pursed her lips as she looked over at him. "I really have nothing else to say."

"I suppose I have worn out my welcome." He looked directly into Joyce's eyes. "Unless of course, Joyce, there's something you'd like to share with me?"

"No, Detective Crackle. It's just a friendly visit."

"A friendly visit with a stranger?" He crossed his arms and looked between both of them.

"Are you policing my visitors now, Detective Crackle? As I told you, the death of a young man is always tragic, but it has nothing to do with me. Nothing at all."

"Nothing." He grunted, then nodded. "All right then, I'll be on my way." He stepped towards the door, then paused just beside Joyce. "Are you sure that you know what you're doing here?"

"Yes, Detective, thank you for your concern."

He stared at her for a moment longer, then turned and walked down the driveway. Mrs. Pierce closed the door behind him.

"I know we're supposed to be friendly to the police, but if his car leaves an oil slick on my driveway, I am going to sue." She huffed and balled her hands into fists. "He was also quite rude. He insisted that I had a relationship with some man that worked in a food truck. Honestly."

"Oh, then you didn't know Adam?" Joyce furrowed a brow.

"Of course I did, but that is certainly nothing the police need to know about. Now, tell me who you are and how you knew Adam." She led her into a small sitting room off the foyer.

"Through business. I own a food truck as well."

"Why are you here exactly?"

"Well, I found a photo of you in his truck, and I wanted to find out the nature of your relationship, if you knew him well," Joyce said casually.

"No, I didn't."

"If you didn't know Adam that well, how did he get a picture of you?" Joyce furrowed a brow.

"Who knows, maybe he was obsessed with me and snapped a picture while he was stalking me." She crossed her arms.

"He mentioned to his friends that he was seeing an older woman. He said that she was the most beautiful woman he'd ever known."

"I have no idea what you're talking about."

"You see, I visited some of his friends, and they mentioned that Adam was seeing someone. The things they said about this person, well, they were a bit scandalous."

"Scandalous?" She clutched at her throat.

"How she's rich, older…"

"People are always spreading rumors about the rich. It's pathetic."

"Yes, of course it is. I figured that's all it was, rumors." Joyce shook her head. "I'm sorry for bothering you."

"Do you have the picture?"

"No, that's why I wanted to warn you, in case things get out."

"Great." She clenched her jaw. "Then the rumors will fly."

"I'm only here to help, Kathy. They said that he said that he loved you."

"Loved me?" She laughed and shook her head. "No, I doubt that very highly. Perhaps he loved my money, though. Oh, don't be uncomfortable. I'm okay with a man loving me for my money. It gets me what I want, and there's nothing wrong with that. Is there?"

"No, I suppose not." Joyce forced a smile. "Anyway, maybe your husband found out about the affair?"

"Not much of a chance of that. My husband and I are barely in the same room together. He wouldn't notice if I moved to another country. Now, I think it's best that you leave."

"Of course, I'll be on my way. Oh, and Kathy?"

"Yes?"

"Do you think if your husband did find out about the affair, he'd be angry enough to kill Adam?"

"I don't think he'd care that much, to be honest." A hint of sadness crossed her face. For just a moment, Joyce felt sorry for her. "It's time for you to go."

"I'll be on my way. But keep in mind, Kathy, if I found out about your relationship, I think it's safe to say that your husband could have found out as well."

"He didn't do this. He wouldn't. He'd never risk going to jail!" Kathy called out just as Joyce closed the door behind her. Maybe she didn't get exactly the information she wanted, but it was enough for the moment. The important thing was that she had stirred the pot, and hopefully it would lead to Kathy or her husband making a big mistake. Now that she had confirmed the affair, Pierce was most certainly on the top of her suspect list.

CHAPTER 14

As Joyce drove down the road away from the Pierce estate, her thoughts were occupied by her encounter with Kathy. When flashing lights appeared behind her, she almost didn't notice them. It wasn't until the shrill shriek of a siren made her jump out of her skin, that she realized she was being pulled over. In the dim light of the evening, she made out that the car behind her was not a marked police car. She recognized the beat-up old vehicle a moment later. With a knot in her stomach, she pulled off to the side of the road and came to a stop. When Detective Crackle walked up to the window of her car, she reluctantly rolled it down.

"What is this all about?"

"I think that's something I should be asking you."

"Because I visited Kathy?"

"Because you know more than you're telling me." He leaned on the frame of the window and looked into her eyes. "What I can't figure out is why you would want to hide things from me? What are you getting out of all of this?"

"Nothing," she said and then looked away from him. "I just want to know what happened to Adam and Pete."

"And I don't?" He wrapped his hand on the door of the car. "I thought you agreed to cooperate."

"Look, I'm sure I don't know anything more than you do. I can only imagine you were there to discuss the affair Adam had with Kathy. Am I wrong?"

"An affair which she denied but you seem to have proof of."

"I actually don't have proof. But Kathy did admit it to me. She didn't seem to think it was such a big deal."

"Clever." He smiled. "I think maybe I should hire you. Are you interested in a badge?"

"No thanks. My late husband was the one who wore a badge."

"Oh, I'm sorry for your loss." He frowned. "I had no idea you were a widow of a police officer."

"Thank you." She cleared her throat.

"Was he killed on duty?"

"No, he had retired." She smiled a little. "Not that he ever really turned in his badge."

"I understand that. Now you seem to be carrying on the tradition."

"I just like to see justice served, Detective Crackle." She gazed at him through the open car window. "I'm really not working against you."

"I'm glad to hear that, because what you just did in there was quite risky. You need to be more careful and as I said before, leave this to me. All right?" He held her gaze and offered a small smile in return.

"Agreed." She nodded to appease him and patted the hand that still rested on her car window. "In the interest of sharing, I think that Pierce should be considered the prime suspect in both murders."

"Pierce? I thought you were hot on Vince?"

"Vince fits the bill, but he seems to have turned into a legitimate businessman. I think Pierce has a lot more to lose than Vince."

"What makes you think that?"

"The affair, the fact that his half-sister owns the

diner on Green Street, and I believe that Cooper was willing to participate in bribery on a small scale while Pierce continued to participate in bribery on a much larger scale. Although Pierce didn't directly take money from the truck owners, he made it possible for Cooper to do so, without fear of getting caught."

"How do you know that?"

"It's a hunch that was partly confirmed when Cooper was prepared to accept a bribe from me. Did you see the Pierce estate? You think he got that from just being a councilman? I don't think so. My guess is Kathy let something slip to Adam about Pierce's business dealings. Adam saw a chance at a payday and tried to blackmail Pierce. Maybe he was worried that Adam would try to stop the rezoning of Green Street. So Pierce killed him to keep his mouth shut and stop him. Not to mention the affair. Maybe when he found out about the affair, it was the final straw and he just wanted to get Adam out of the picture."

"I will look into it." He nodded as he stepped away from her car.

"Thank you, Detective Crackle." She smiled at him for a moment, then started her car. As she drove away, she hoped that he meant what he said. All of the investigating in the world would mean nothing if he didn't support it.

As soon as Joyce arrived at home, her phone began to ring.

"Hello?"

"Joyce!"

"Brenda, don't be upset."

"How can I not be?"

"I guess Charlie told you?"

"Joyce, this has to stop. You can't do this alone."

"Listen, I need you to stop worrying about me so much. I get that to you I'm just a frail old lady…"

"That's not true at all."

"Good. So, do you want to join me tomorrow?"

"What are your plans?"

"I'm going to speak to Pierce again."

"But I thought you were convinced he is the murderer?"

"I am. But he is also the local councilman. We have a right to speak to him, just as any other concerned citizen does."

"All right, I'm in. But we should do it in a public place."

"Why not the diner?"

"That's perfect. When we reveal that we know his sister owns the place, that should knock him right off balance. Then we can ask him some more inflammatory questions and see how he reacts."

"Okay, that sounds like it might work, or perhaps get us thrown out of the restaurant." Joyce chuckled.

"Either way, we'll certainly get a reaction."

"I'll place the call first thing in the morning."

"How do you know that he'll meet with us?"

"Trust me, I'll get him to come to the table." She hung up the phone and spent the rest of the evening deciding what she would say to Pierce.

～

The next morning Joyce looked through her contacts list to find Pierce's number. After the protest, she was sure she was the last person he wanted to hear from, but once she told him what she knew, she doubted he would risk turning down the meeting. First, she would try to coax him in with a little honey. As the phone rang, she took a few slow breaths and willed confidence into her voice.

"Councilman Pierce's office. May I help you?"

"Yes, I'd like to invite Councilman Pierce to lunch today."

"I'm not sure that will be possible, as he has a very busy schedule."

"Please let him know that it is Joyce, from Green Street, and I'd like to talk with him about Adam."

"Okay, hold please."

A few moments later, a new voice came on the phone.

"Joyce. First you stage a protest against me, and now you want to invite me to lunch? Do you think I'm some kind of fool?"

"Not at all. I am very sorry about the protest. I had my facts confused. I wish I hadn't been so quick to react. That's part of the reason I'd like to invite you to lunch. I want to apologize again for being misinformed."

"Oh?" He paused. "I suppose that's a good start."

"Oh, absolutely. And also, I'd like to discuss Melvin with you."

"Melvin?"

"Yes, he's made me an offer that's very troubling to me. He says that Adam was given the same offer. Now that I know that you are as honest as they come, I'm hoping you can help me decide what to do about this."

"I'm not sure how I can help you with that."

"Well, you see, Melvin told me that if I pay him…"

"Wait, it might be better if we discuss this at lunch." He cleared his throat. "Phone calls are so impersonal."

"Yes, you're absolutely right. Plus, you never can be certain of who is listening, can you, Councilman?"

"Right." He sighed. "About twelve?"

"Yes, twelve it is. At the diner would be the best place, I think. You know it, don't you? The one on the corner?"

"Uh, sure. Okay, that's fine. I'll be there."

"Thanks for taking time out of your busy schedule."

"Anything for a valued citizen."

Joyce smirked as she hung up the phone. The moment she hinted at Melvin offering to accept a bribe, he'd become more than eager to meet with her. That meant, as she suspected, that Pierce more than likely knew all about the bribes Melvin was taking. Was he worried that she was going to expose him not only as a dodgy politician, but also a murderer?

～

*J*oyce and Brenda arrived at the diner fifteen minutes early and chose their table so that it would be secluded from the rest of the restaurant. The waitress offered them a brighter smile this time, but Joyce wasn't in the mood to smile back. She was nervous.

"So when he gets here, we need to press him about his involvement in the closure of Green Street."

"Okay, we're ready for this." Brenda nodded. "The worst that can happen is he proves that he isn't the murderer, and then we'll be back to square one."

"Right." Joyce glanced at her watch. "At least we have some time."

"Or maybe not." Brenda tipped her head towards the door. Joyce looked over to see Councilman Pierce stride through it. He locked eyes on them then headed straight for their table. The powerful way he walked, and the cold expression he wore, was enough to send a shiver through Joyce. Yes, she could easily see him as a killer.

"All right, I'm here." He sat down at the table with them and smoothed down his tie. "I hope you're not planning on wasting my time again. I have many people to see today. I just want to get the details of our business ironed out."

"First, there are a few things I want to know." Joyce folded her hands on the table between them.

"What?" Pierce asked.

"How much would you get out of it if Green Street was rezoned?"

"Not this again. I have no idea what you are talking about."

"I think you do. I think Adam got mad when he found out you were trying to get rid of the food trucks on Green Street. He'd just had a new partner invest in his business, he was expanding. You would have cost Adam a lot of money, enough to make him confront you about what he knew."

"I think you've overplayed your hand here." He shook his head. "You do realize that nothing you say can be proven, right? As I said before, you are mistaken. Why would I want to do anything to get rid of the food trucks?"

"Maybe because your half-sister owns this diner and you don't want her to lose money anymore. If Green Street is closed to food trucks, she will make a killing."

"Maybe you don't know what you're talking

about." He shook his head. "I knew this was a mistake."

"What I couldn't figure out is why Adam and Pete needed to die in all of this. I mean, so you want to be a shady businessman, fine, that's not unusual. But did Adam and Pete really need to die?"

"I had nothing to do with that." He gritted his teeth as he glared at her.

"I think Adam found out all about the diner, and he was furious. You were worried that if Adam told the other truck owners the truth about your plans and managed to get them to join forces and try to stop the rezoning, all of it would unravel. So you did what you had to do, didn't you?"

"What am I supposed to do now, confess?" He held up his hands and laughed. "No way. I had nothing to do with that. You two might think that you're detectives, but you're not very good ones. Okay, you figured out about my sister owning the diner, but that doesn't mean I had anything to do with Adam and Pete being killed. Not as clever as you thought. Are you?" He stood up from the table. "Did you think you'd come in here with your little bits of information and turn me into a blathering child?" He smirked. "You're not equipped for the big league, ladies. Perhaps you owe me an apology?"

"Perhaps." Joyce stood up as well. "But you're not going to get one."

"Risky." He straightened his tie. "I guess you don't intend to do any more business in this city in the future. Hmm?"

"I intend to." Joyce wagged her finger as she spoke. "With an honest councilman, not one that is willing to overlook bribery, push for the rezoning against citizens' wishes for personal gain, and might be involved in the murder of two citizens."

"If you continue to suggest that I am involved in the murder of Adam and Pete, I'm going to begin to take offense to it." He chuckled. "Those comments could really leave a mark."

"Let's go, Joyce. There's nothing more we can do here." Brenda guided her towards the door.

"This isn't the end, Councilman." Joyce shot a glare over her shoulder.

"If you say so." He smiled and watched as they left the restaurant. As soon as they were outside, Joyce looked at Brenda.

"We need to stop him."

"I know, Joyce, but we're not going to get him to confess anything. He never admitted to the bribes or confirmed his intentions to shut down Green Street. He danced around everything. Besides, even if he was involved in all of this, it doesn't prove he's a murderer."

"I can tell you this much, I'm not going to let him scare me. Tomorrow morning I'm going to be at the truck. You don't have to be, but I'm going to be there."

"I will be there, too. Remember, we're in this together."

CHAPTER 15

*J*oyce lay awake in bed even though it was well past three in the morning. She couldn't get her mind to calm down enough to fall asleep. She kept re-running the conversation with Pierce through her mind. But no matter how hard she tried, she couldn't think of enough evidence that would call for him to be arrested. Maybe he was slippery enough to get away with murder. Finally, she gave up on trying to sleep and sat down in front of her computer instead. She realized she had a new email from Brenda.

When I arrived home last night, Charlie told me he had set up the camera on the truck like we had planned. He set it up with a video feed to his computer and he turned it on to test it. He caught Vince talking to someone near the truck. I thought you might be able to tell what they're saying to fill in some of the blanks. Let me know what you think.

Brenda

Joyce began to review the video. Although she could tell on the camera that it was Vince, even though a hat covered his features, a tall figure that stood near him kept going in and out of the camera shot. He was wearing a long coat and a hat pulled low to cover his features. She couldn't see his face to lip read. Due to the hat Vince wore, a shadow hung over his upper face, but she could see his lips. She watched it a few times and tried to lip read what she could of what Vince said.

"Are you sure?" Vince asked.

She could see the other man nodding as he spoke.

"But this is bad," Vince said. "When?"

Joyce wished that she could see what the other man was saying.

"But there might be a problem."

The man pointed his finger threateningly at Vince, and then he turned and walked away.

Soon after, Vince walked away as well. Although there was nothing overtly incriminating on the video, Joyce's skin crawled with the possibilities of what it meant. She replayed the video and tried to piece together a few more words. As her stomach churned with what the man in the film and Vince's intentions might be, she discerned more from the man's forceful body language than she did from anything else.

On a whim, Joyce attached the video file to an email and sent it off to Detective Crackle. In the body of the email, she asked if he had any idea who the shadowy figure in the image was. Still too riled up to sleep, she got dressed for the day and made an early breakfast. When she looked at the clock again, it was nearly six. She would be at the truck early, but it was better than staring into space. At least if she went to the truck, she could do some organizing and cleaning with all of her nervous energy.

On her way there, she observed the city beginning to wake up. There were plenty of taxis on the road and even more people walking down the sidewalks that lined the towering buildings. When she arrived at Green Street, all of the trucks that lined the road were still dark and quiet. She noticed some people near one of the shops that was being renovated and thought she saw Cooper walking out of it. What was he doing at the shop? Maybe she was mistaken. It was still dark and he was far away. She parked in her usual spot and made her way towards the truck. As she approached it, she heard a noise near the dumpster. Her heart skipped a beat. She turned her head in the direction of the dumpster and was suddenly struck by something heavy. She struggled to stay on her feet, but darkness swept over her.

~

*B*renda finished brushing her hair, then peeked in at Sophie asleep in her bed. She still had a little time before she had to wake up for school. Still, she couldn't resist placing a light kiss on the top of her head. When she poked her head into Charlie's office, he was hard at work. She stepped away from the door so as not to interrupt him.

"Brenda?" He smiled as he caught her eye.

"Morning, sweetie. I didn't want to distract you."

"You never have to worry about that. You're always a welcome distraction." He kissed her, then met her eyes. "Are you going in soon?"

"Yes, after a quick breakfast, I'm sure Joyce will be eager to figure out our next step."

"Okay, be careful. Did Joyce ever get back to you about the footage?"

"Not yet, I'm sure she'll tell me once I get there."

"I don't like that guy lurking around your truck." Charlie frowned.

"I know, me neither. Have you checked the feed this morning?"

"It seems to be off. I knew I should have bought the more expensive one. Call me when you get there and I can walk you through resetting it."

"Okay, I will. But try not to worry. I'll be just fine."

"I'll try." He held her gaze a moment longer before he turned his attention back to his work.

As Brenda made herself a quick breakfast, she sent a text to Joyce.

Good morning. I'll be at the truck soon. Running a bit late.

They always sent a text to each other if they were running late. While she ate her toast and drank her coffee, she waited for a text in return. When she didn't receive one, she tossed out the remainder of her toast and finished getting ready. If Joyce wasn't awake yet, she would be very late. Brenda wanted to be sure she was there in time to get things going and everything ready before it was time to open up.

Brenda glanced at her watch, then at her phone. It seemed odd that she hadn't heard anything back from Joyce. As she walked out to the car, she wondered if maybe she'd overslept or decided to sleep in. It was unusual, but she hadn't been sleeping well lately. She drove towards the truck. At every red light she checked her phone, but by the time she arrived at Green Street, she still hadn't received a text in return. After a few moments of consideration, she decided to open up the truck, then call to check on Joyce. As she turned into the parking lot, her heart lurched. There in its usual spot was Joyce's car. She dialed Joyce's number right away. The phone rang several times, then went to voicemail.

"Joyce? Where are you? I'm worried about you. Call me when you get this." She hung up and dialed the number again as she walked towards the truck. Again the phone began to ring, but this time, she could hear it ringing nearby, not far from the truck. She followed the sound of the ringing phone towards the dumpster. "Joyce? Are you there?" With the sun just rising, the street was still filled with shadows. The eerie sound of Joyce's phone ringing was the only thing that broke the quiet. Brenda shivered as a chill raced up her spine. She forced herself to take a step closer to the dumpster. If Joyce was hurt and couldn't answer her, then every second would count. As she swung the lid of the dumpster open, she was struck by something heavy on the back of her head, then everything went black.

When Brenda opened her eyes again, she instantly realized her hands were tied.

"Help!" She peered through the darkness.

"Brenda?" Joyce's voice was thin and a few inches away from her.

"Joyce!" Brenda twisted her head and saw her friend, whose hands were also bound. "Where are we? What happened?"

"I don't know." She blinked and tried to see clearly through the dim lighting. "I don't know. I can't tell. It's too dark."

"We have to get out of here." Brenda wiggled until she was closer to Joyce. "Here, let me get at the rope, I might be able to untie you."

"Hurry." Joyce's heart raced. "I have a bad feeling about this."

"I can get it, it's not too tight." Brenda tugged at the rope until it pulled free.

Joyce staggered to her feet then bent down to

untie Brenda's ropes. "Let's go, we need to get out fast, before whoever struck us comes back."

"All right. Ouch, my head hurts." A wave of dizziness washed over Brenda as she stood up.

The two women leaned on each other as they headed for the only door in sight.

CHAPTER 16

The old beat-up car pulled into the parking lot. It eased to a stop near two parked cars. The driver grabbed a handheld radio and spoke into it.

"Their cars are here, but still no response on either cell phone. The truck doesn't look open, I'm going to check it out." He stepped out of the car just as another vehicle squealed into the parking lot. Charlie bolted out of the car and ran straight for Detective Crackle.

"Where are they? Have you found them? Brenda still isn't answering!"

"Not yet, I'm on my way to check the truck. Just try to stay calm, Charlie, we don't know that anything bad has happened." Detective Crackle took a step towards the donut truck, and in that instant, the truck exploded. The ground rocked, a few nearby windows shattered, and several other trucks took some damage from the flying pieces of metal. People in the area scattered for cover. While most ran away from the truck, Charlie lunged towards it.

"No!" Charlie rushed forward, but Detective Crackle grabbed his arm and held him back.

"Don't, Charlie. There's nothing you can do."

"Let me go, Brenda is in there!"

"Charlie, do you think she would want you to risk your life? What about Sophie?" Detective Crackle struggled to hold on to him, but Charlie broke free of his grasp and ran straight for the truck. "Charlie, wait!" Detective Crackle barked some commands into his radio, then ran after him. The truck was decimated by the blast. Charlie fell to his knees as he looked at the still-burning rubble.

"How did I let this happen?"

"Charlie, we don't know that they were in there." Detective Crackle rested a hand on his shoulder.

"Where else could they be? Where?" Charlie forced himself to his feet.

"Right here! I'm right here, Charlie!" Brenda

ran towards him and threw her arms around him. Joyce was a few steps behind her.

"Brenda!" Charlie held her close. "Oh, thank goodness!"

Joyce stood close to the pair and gazed at the remains of the truck. Her heart slammed against her chest. As she stared at it, she remembered seeing Cooper walking out of one of the shops that was being renovated. Everything suddenly fell into place.

"It was never Pierce, it was always Cooper." Joyce shook her head.

"Care to fill me in on all of this?" Detective Crackle wrapped an arm around her shoulders.

"Someone knocked us both out and tied us up! It's a rather long story." She frowned.

"I have time."

"No, you don't. You need to be arresting Cooper right this second."

"Officers are out looking for him. After you sent me that footage, along with what you thought was being said, I pulled in a favor and asked someone to enhance it. I saw that it was Cooper. I went to speak to Mrs. Cooper to question her about her husband. She got herself into a bit of a bind with her lies and admitted that she lied about shopping with him to give him an alibi. After I found that out, I decided to check on you. At the same time Charlie called me, panicking that Brenda wasn't answering the phone. He had found out that Cooper owned part of a company that was listed as one of the investors that purchased the shops on Green Street. He was going to turn them into restaurants. We both rushed over here, and when I saw the truck blow, I sent out an order to pick up Cooper," Detective Crackle said. "I just need the proof that it was Cooper."

"Well, I don't have any." Joyce sighed.

"But I do." Vince walked up to them with his hands held high in the air. "I'm the one that knocked you out and tied you up."

"What?" Joyce spun around to face him.

"Keep your hands up!" Detective Crackle drew his weapon.

"I know, I know. I look like the bad guy here. But for once, I did something right. Cooper came to me, said he wanted me to solve a problem for him." Vince kept his hands up.

"Let me guess, the problem was us?" Joyce frowned.

"Yes, it was."

"It looks like we can get the story directly from him." Detective Crackle signaled towards two uniformed officers that were walking towards him. Cooper was in handcuffs between them, struggling to get out of their grasp.

"We found him around the corner, Detective," the taller officer said.

"I am not saying anything." Cooper shook his head.

"You don't need to, I know everything." Vince smirked.

"You keep your mouth shut!" Cooper demanded.

"You killed Adam. I am not a sentimental person, but we had plans together that I now have to change. Then you tried to kill me. I am not keeping anything shut." Vince scowled.

"You traitor!" Cooper shouted at Vince. "You liar, I did nothing!"

"No, you're the liar. I think we are even now. You were going to kill me!"

"Take him to the station." Detective Crackle looked towards the officers holding Cooper.

"You're making a mistake. I had nothing to do with this!" Cooper shouted as the officers led him to the waiting patrol car.

"What happened?" Detective Crackle looked at Vince.

"It turns out that he wouldn't get his hands dirty when it came to you two. I told him that I needed to know all of the details. I guess that Adam had a real thing for Pierce's wife and thought by exposing the truth about the bribes and the reason why he was pushing to rezone Green Street, it might get rid of Pierce and Cooper and he would have a chance with her. Adam found out that Cooper had bought those two shops on Green Street to turn them into restaurants."

"I bet that Kathy told Adam all about the diner and the shops and the rezoning while they were snuggled up together, and Adam was furious. Cooper knew that if Adam told the other truck owners the truth about his plans, all of it would unravel. So, he did what he had to do? He thought killing him would keep him quiet?" Joyce shook her head.

"I think you're right. Anyway, Cooper tried to convince Adam to keep quiet, but he was all in his face about morals and honesty. A bit ironic don't you think, considering Adam was sleeping with Pierce's wife. Apparently, Pierce didn't care about the affairs, because it kept her out of his hair. Pierce had said to Cooper that there was nothing to worry about. Anyway, from what I understand, when

Adam got on his moral high ground with Cooper, he lost his temper. Cooper grabbed the hot dog bin lid and hit him over the head."

"What about Pete?" Detective Crackle asked.

"Pete started asking too many questions. So, Cooper killed him, too. Only this time he was more prepared and brought his gun. Cooper was furious with Pierce because of Kathy. Cooper said that Pierce wanted more money, but wouldn't do what was necessary to get it. Pierce had nothing to do with the murders. Cooper wanted me to do his dirty work. Maybe he didn't want to kill the two of you himself. Or maybe he just wanted to get rid of me, too. He said he needed me to take care of you two for him."

"And you didn't go to the cops?" Charlie took a step forward, but Detective Crackle put a hand out to restrain him.

"Of course not. Hey, it was a free payday, I wasn't going to argue. I figured I'd take the cash, let him think I did it, then turn him in once I had the money stashed somewhere."

"What exactly happened?" Detective Crackle asked Vince. "Did he tell you to come here?"

"Cooper said to wait for Joyce and Brenda in the truck." Vince smirked. "Look, I wasn't ever going to off you two, that's not my style. But when he told me to be in that truck, that was when I knew."

"Knew what?" Joyce stared at him.

"He was making a clean sweep. Somehow, he found out Adam and I were partners, and he must have suspected that Adam might have told me something. He didn't want me to live either. When he said for me to be in the truck, I guessed that he was planning something that would take out all three of us. So, I hooked the camera on the truck up to my own phone and watched him set up a bomb under the truck. I didn't know when it would go off, if it was rigged to the door, or timed, or pressure sensitive. I was going to call the police with an anonymous tip, but Joyce got here before I could. She was headed right for the truck, and I knew she was scared of me, so if she saw me, she might run for it. I didn't want the old gal to get blown to bits, so I knocked her out and tied her up to keep her from heading for the truck when she woke up. Again, I was about to call the police, but then along came Brenda here, so I had to do the same to her. I stuck them in one of the empty shops. I know, it might not have been pleasant, but it's more pleasant than being in that truck. I have the proof of Cooper planting the bomb. I have it all recorded." He tilted his head towards the remains. "He expected all three of us to be in there."

"You saved us?" Brenda stared at him.

"I guess." He shrugged.

"If it weren't for you, Vince, we'd be dead," Joyce said.

"Try not to forget that this man also knocked you out! There had to be other options." Detective Crackle put him in cuffs and turned him around to face Joyce.

"No, that wasn't the greatest choice." She rubbed the back of her head. "But he's right. I would have run for the truck the moment I saw him."

"And I would have, too." Brenda pulled away from Charlie enough to look at Vince. "Thank you."

"Vince, you're under arrest, at least until we get this all figured out," Detective Crackle said.

"I expected that." Vince shrugged. "But I couldn't let this happen."

As Detective Crackle led Vince away to the arriving patrol cars, Brenda and Joyce looked at each other.

"I guess the truth will come out now, about Cooper and Pierce, and all the bribes and dodgy business deals. I'm sure now that this has all been revealed Pierce will have to face the consequences of his actions." Joyce shook her head. "I mean I suspected Cooper was a shady businessman, but I can't believe he was the murderer. I guess Pierce was telling the truth after all."

"About one thing at least," Brenda said.

"And Vince saved us." Joyce widened her eyes.

"What about the truck?"

"I have good insurance." Joyce smiled. "And we needed a new oven anyway."

"Yes, we sure did!" Brenda laughed. "I guess that's one good thing that came out of all of this."

"I guess so." Joyce sighed. She was glad the murders were solved, and that Green Street would remain open for business, but she wished it hadn't cost two lives. For his greed, Melvin Cooper would be locked away for a long time, she was sure of it, and one day soon Green Street would return to business as usual. They would find a way to move forward, one donut at a time.

The End

CHOCOLATE GLAZED DONUTS WITH SPRINKLES

Ingredients:

Donuts:

1 cup milk

1/3 cup granulated sugar

1 packet active dry yeast

3 tablespoons butter

1/2 teaspoon salt

2 egg yolks at room temperature

2 1/2 cups bread flour plus extra for rolling

1/2 teaspoon nutmeg

1 teaspoon vanilla extract

Vegetable oil for frying

Glaze:

4 ounces semi-sweet chocolate
1 cup confectioners' sugar
2 tablespoons milk plus extra to thin the glaze if
necessary
1 teaspoon vanilla extract

Sprinkles for decorating

Preparation:

Prepare a baking tray by oiling it and set aside.
Line another baking tray with paper towels and
set aside.

Heat the milk until warm. Put the warm milk, sugar
and yeast in a bowl and leave aside until the mixture
starts frothing. This should take about 10 - 15
minutes.

Melt the butter and leave aside to cool.

Add the butter, salt, egg yolks, flour, nutmeg and
vanilla extract to the milk and yeast mixture and
mix until combined.

With lightly floured hands knead the dough on a floured surface until smooth.

Place the dough in an oiled bowl and cover with plastic wrap.

Leave in a warm place for about an hour until almost doubled in size.

On a floured surface punch back the dough then knead until smooth.

Using a floured rolling pin roll the dough to about half an inch thick and then using a donut cutter cut out the donuts.

Take the off-cuts and roll out again and cut. It should make about 12 donut holes and donuts. Place the donuts on the oiled baking tray.

Cover with plastic wrap and leave in a warm area for about 30 minutes until almost doubled in size.

Using a deep fryer or Dutch oven heat the oil to 350 degrees Fahrenheit. Use a deep-fry thermometer to check the temperature if using a Dutch oven.

Fry the donuts and donut holes in batches. Fry for about a minute on each side until golden brown. Put the donuts on the paper lined baking tray and cool slightly.

For the glaze melt the chocolate preferably in a double boiler.

When the chocolate is melted add the confectioners' sugar, milk and vanilla extract and whisk vigorously until well combined.

If the mixture is too thick gradually add a bit more milk until it is the right consistency.

When it is at the right consistency leave it aside to cool slightly.

Dip the tops of the donuts into the glaze, then dip them into the sprinkles.

Leave on a plate to set.

Enjoy!

ALSO BY CINDY BELL

Tea Can Be Deadly

Greed Can Be Deadly

Clutter Can Be Deadly

WAGGING TAIL COZY MYSTERIES

Murder at Pooch Park

Murder at the Pet Boutique

CHOCOLATE CENTERED COZY MYSTERIES

The Sweet Smell of Murder

A Deadly Delicious Delivery

A Bitter Sweet Murder

A Treacherous Tasty Trail

Pastry and Peril

Trouble and Treats

Fudge Films and Felonies

Custom-Made Murder

Skydiving, Soufflés and Sabotage

Christmas Chocolates and Crimes

Hot Chocolate and Homicide

Chocolate Caramels and Conmen

Picnics, Pies and Lies

DUNE HOUSE COZY MYSTERIES

Seaside Secrets

Boats and Bad Guys

Treasured History

Hidden Hideaways

Dodgy Dealings

Suspects and Surprises

Ruffled Feathers

A Fishy Discovery

Danger in the Depths

Celebrities and Chaos

Pups, Pilots and Peril

Tides, Trails and Trouble

Racing and Robberies

Athletes and Alibis

BEKKI THE BEAUTICIAN COZY MYSTERIES

Hairspray and Homicide

A Dyed Blonde and a Dead Body

Mascara and Murder

Pageant and Poison

Conditioner and a Corpse

Mistletoe, Makeup and Murder

Hairpin, Hair Dryer and Homicide

Blush, a Bride and a Body

Shampoo and a Stiff

Cosmetics, a Cruise and a Killer

Lipstick, a Long Iron and Lifeless

Camping, Concealer and Criminals

Treated and Dyed

A Wrinkle-Free Murder

A MACARON PATISSERIE COZY MYSTERY SERIES

Sifting for Suspects

Recipes and Revenge

Mansions, Macarons and Murder

NUTS ABOUT NUTS COZY MYSTERIES

A Tough Case to Crack

A Seed of Doubt

Roasted Penuts and Peril

HEAVENLY HIGHLAND INN COZY MYSTERIES

Murdering the Roses

Dead in the Daisies

Killing the Carnations

Drowning the Daffodils

Suffocating the Sunflowers

Books, Bullets and Blooms

A Deadly Serious Gardening Contest

A Bridal Bouquet and a Body

Digging for Dirt

WENDY THE WEDDING PLANNER COZY
MYSTERIES

Matrimony, Money and Murder

Chefs, Ceremonies and Crimes

Knives and Nuptials

Mice, Marriage and Murder

ABOUT THE AUTHOR

Cindy Bell is a USA Today and Wall Street Journal Bestselling Author. She is the author of the cozy mystery series Wagging Tail, Donut Truck, Dune House, Sage Gardens, Chocolate Centered, Macaron Patisserie, Nuts about Nuts, Bekki the Beautician, Heavenly Highland Inn and Wendy the Wedding Planner.

Cindy has always loved reading, but it is only recently that she has discovered her passion for writing romantic cozy mysteries. She loves walking along the beach thinking of the next adventure her characters can embark on.

You can sign up for her newsletter so you are notified of her latest releases at http://www.cindybellbooks.com.